Books by Geoffrey Household

NOVELS

The Third Hour	*Watcher in the Shadows*
Rogue Male	*Thing to Love*
Arabesque	*Olura*
The High Place	*The Courtesy of Death*
A Rough Shoot	*Dance of the Dwarfs*
A Time to Kill	*Doom's Caravan*
Fellow Passenger	*The Three Sentinels*

AUTOBIOGRAPHY

Against the Wind

SHORT STORIES

The Salvation of Pisco Gabar
Tale of Adventurers
The Brides of Solomon and Other Stories
Sabres on the Sand

FOR CHILDREN

The Exploits of Xenophon
The Spanish Cave
Prisoner of the Indies

The Three Sentinels

THE
THREE SENTINELS
BY GEOFFREY HOUSEHOLD

AN ATLANTIC MONTHLY PRESS BOOK
Little, Brown and Company—Boston—Toronto

LIBRARY OF CONGRESS CATALOG CARD NO. 74–186961

FIRST EDITION

T 05/72

ATLANTIC–LITTLE, BROWN BOOKS
ARE PUBLISHED BY
LITTLE, BROWN AND COMPANY
IN ASSOCIATION WITH
THE ATLANTIC MONTHLY PRESS

Published simultaneously in Canada
by Little, Brown & Company (Canada) Limited

PRINTED IN THE UNITED STATES OF AMERICA

The Three Sentinels

ONE. That coast had none of the exhilaration of savagery. The spent swell of the Pacific broke on the beach in parallel lines with the regularity of a vast body radiating into empty space. Above the high tidemark of some long-forgotten storm the gray-brown sand turned to gray-brown soil with no clear line of demarcation; and this barren plain extended inland for a couple of miles until the first ridge of the Andes sprang from it so exactly that in places a builder's set square could have been pushed into the angle. It was a coast forbidding habitation, resembling some imaginary reconstruction of Permian landscape; but not even the most desperate of amphibians would have attempted to experiment upon that still and utterly waterless land.

The desolation curiously affected those who were at ease in it. They regarded their home, so far as it permitted itself to be loved at all, with the proud perversion of islanders. Their irrigated patch in the midst of the dry detritus of sea and mountains was as startling and unnatural as the white esplanades, further along the coast, of the sea birds' colonies. The green became a symbol of protection. So perhaps was white to the gulls.

The ridge which rose from the coastal plain was barren as it had been before the coming of the oil company except for the black road which swept up it in three long legs forming an easy gradient for the monstrous truckloads of drill pipe and casing. Here and there a boulder, loosened from the crest by wind, stood immovable among packed gravel, though to the eye off balance. The only lump of organic life, vaguely black and white, where Rafael Garay squatted on the hillside with his arm around his son, adjusted itself to gravity with more ease.

Immediately below him were the whitewashed, red-roofed cottages of the labor lines dotted by cans and pots of dusty flowers. Further north a green strip of cultivated land ran along the coast, protected by groves of eucalyptus where at last it met the desert. To the south was the Company town, the sheds, dumps and wharves of the port and the two breakwaters against which the Pacific, every twenty seconds, spurted its spray to precisely the same height. Beyond the port, after a green interlude of sports grounds, the desert returned, made still more desolate by acres of concrete in which were set the power station, the refinery and the shining metal masses of the tank farm. There all evidence of human life ended except for some shacks close to the garbage-strewn beach left over from the very early days of the Company.

Rafael Garay had left his bed at first light, resentful of the unaccustomed responsibilities of leadership. To be in the midst of talk was inspiring; it clarified the thought of the speaker as well as that of the committee or audience which listened. But between the talking of yesterday and the talking of today, so much of it unnecessary, one felt the need of self-forgetfulness. That was why he had tiptoed out of his house to the refreshment of dawn.

He had not realized that the big eyes of his son were open and watching him. When he reached his perch on the ridge and turned round the beloved figure was trotting up doggedly after him. He ran down and lifted the boy in his arms with passionate Latin paternity. It was needless to ask him why he had followed. The boy remained at his side, silent and half asleep.

Far out over the melancholy crawlings of the Pacific, clouds had become radiant though the shore was still held under the Cordillera's overpowering shadow. In the half-world a cock crew. There was a stirring in the nearest group of houses: the susurration of a hive of men and women laying aside their blankets and lighting fires. Underlying this faint chant of human sounds was the distant drone of the overflow from the Charca: a thin column of water arching down from the wall of the reservoir into

5

the pool which fed the irrigation channels a hundred feet below. Rafael was suddenly exasperated by the blankness of this smooth, inverted triangle of concrete which blocked the mouth of the only ravine. Colorless in the dawn it advertised the will, finance and technical intelligence of the Compañía Petrolífera Cabo Desierto. Without it neither the cultivated land nor the future he planned for himself and his fellows was possible. He knew that. Still, such power was indecent.

Peace? There wasn't any peace apart from the boy. The calm of the port below him was that of a corpse. Two of the Company's tankers were tied up far away in the Capital, idle. The third rode high at the offshore buoys. No oil flowed except from the tank farm to the power station. And for all this he, Rafael Garay, was largely responsible. He admitted to himself that a man who killed could not expect peace. It was enough to be satisfied that one was in the right.

He was a carpenter, and by trial and error had become a craftsman. The obstinate genes of Basque ancestors had persisted through passive wombs of Indian and Negro mothers, but he was, to a European eye, black. Since all his society was colored in darkish shades of brown he was unconscious of any major difference. As for his native Indian blood, he insisted without any evidence at all that he was the descendant of princes. That was the Spaniard in him.

Whatever order he was given he could carry out promptly and even wisely; but for all his pride he could not feel the equal of these technicians who created a home in the desert, who drilled beneath the Andes for four kilometers and controlled with such exactitude the ferocities of pressure that oil could be turned on and off as if it were water. They thought of everything before it happened. That was it. If you could think of a thing before it happened you were one of them.

He was not in the least jealous of the pay and privileges of these experts whose bungalows were just over the crest of the ridge behind him. Most of them were British; some were from his own and neighboring republics. All were the same in the essential, seeming to have been born among machinery. How was it possible that men could know so much when they were careless of so much? They even kept acres of grass cut short and wasted their time playing with balls on it instead of feeding it to animals. Some could hardly speak Spanish or work with their own hands. Yet their technology formed a gulf more impassable than that between landowner and peón. There the gulf was merely a difference of income; in all which mattered, dignity and humanity, the peón was the equal of his employer.

He envied only superior knowledge. If it depended on him, there would be no limit to the earnings of men who could do what these had done. No, what he resented was the smooth and cruel world of their creation in which a man was well-meaningly treated as a unit in a mass. Twenty years ago you could fight the Company; now the Company did not seem to be there to fight. The Company approved of the State, and the State of the Company, and men found that between the pair of them they had forfeited all their rights. Cared for like expensive cattle! If you fatten them up you have the right to drive them to market.

The boy in his own way was also reviewing a problem:

7

that though the world was uniformly satisfying there were things in it which ended. He was seven years old and promised to have the same square, powerful face as his father. His skin was much whiter, and he would have passed as a boy from the south of Spain if it had not been for the exceptional grubbiness, unnoticed by a father's eye, of his blue shirt and once-white cotton trousers.

"What *is* death?" he asked suddenly.

The question startled Rafael. He knew that the boy, deep down, mourned for his mother without words either spoken or clearly thought; yet this single bubble bursting at the surface seemed so obviously derived from his own thoughts of the killing of the Company.

"Man, one moment one is here. The next moment one is not."

"But could you die now? Here?"

He was about to answer: yes. But what the devil? A kid must not be left with a thought like that. Deprived of a mother, he couldn't be allowed to believe that he might have no father.

"No, that is impossible," Rafael answered, begging whatever powers might be listening to pay no attention to his reply.

"Why?"

"Because I have so much to do."

"Me, too. Every day I have much to do."

"Indeed?"

"More than when our mother was here."

"How? You used to help her."

"But now I do anything I like. They say: 'Let him alone, poor kid! He has no mother.' "

8

He imitated in miniature the tone and rhythm of some kindly voice intervening in his favor.

"Don't you miss her then?"

That was too solemn and forlorn a thought to be answered at all. The boy countered it with another question.

"They say she was murdered. Who killed her?"

No one. By God, that was the trouble! How easy if there had been any single person who had killed her, if there had been, for example, a boss who could be killed himself or even a boss who would weep at his mistake and beg and be granted forgiveness! But what had killed her was the Company, the State, the Union, the slimy cleverness of a lot of whore's spawn upon none of whom could be placed the sole responsibility.

Up to a point a man of good will could have no complaint. The Company had drilled their three stupendous wells. The whole field had taken pride in the joint triumph of the Three Sentinels which could, it was said, produce two million tons of oil a year for thirty years. So it was reasonable that the Company should decide to close down the old bailing and pumping wells in the shallow field and dismiss eight hundred and seventy men. Clearly there was no longer work for them. But Cabo Desierto was more than an oil field; it had become a home, a *pueblo* like any other with its own shops and streets and taverns and a mayor.

Of the eight hundred and seventy, some four hundred had been willing enough for a change. Either they were young men who were eager to see the rest of the Republic and cared no more for one place than another, or they were Indians resigned to obey. But four hundred and seventy petitioned the Company to be allowed to stay. They were

9

prepared to pay rent for their houses, their share of the communal lands and their water. Impossible, the Company said. Yet they could have made a living from the land — poor, but at least as good as that of any peasant holding up in the Cordillera. That too was reasonable, wasn't it? They refused to go. Why should they go?

Then the Company sent for a *señorito* from the Ministry of Labor to talk to them. He spoke very well — that must be admitted — but like a schoolteacher to children. There was work for all, he said, in the forests or on the new roads or in the steel mill which was being constructed in the south. The country had need of all its faithful sons, and wages would be no less.

"But this faithful son wants to stay where he is. Look, man! Cabo Desierto is our home."

That was Gil Delgado. His father had been an immigrant from Aragon in Spain and Gil was argumentative like all of them. A mastermind but without manners even to his mates.

The *señorito* from the Ministry explained with much patience that there would be no homes in Cabo Desierto if the Company had not made them.

"And there would be no homes from Chile to Mexico," Gil had said, "if the Spaniards had not made them. But that does not mean that we must all go and live in China."

Yet the only answer he got was that the Company could not keep four hundred and seventy extra hands who must be fed though there was no work for them. The State had need of labor and the Company had not. Four hundred and seventy men must do what they were told by the eight million citizens of the country. That was democracy.

The delegate of the Union agreed with him. He agreed with everybody. He admitted that it was all very hard, but the Company had been correct and the Union would see that the State was generous. He was so eloquent that he sprayed spittle on his coat where it shone in the sun like piss on a palm leaf.

Rafael was not immediately concerned, for he was one of those to be retained. Not for his own value. He knew that. The carpenters' shop would have less work now that there was little rigging to be done. No, it was for Catalina that the Company held on to him. Catalina helped Dr. Solano in the hospital. She had only a bit of training in first aid and midwifery, but she was an angel. How many times had the women cried out that they would not be touched till Catalina came! The world had few women like Catalina.

It had been an open meeting down at the port where he and Gil had first protested against this nonsense. Rafael was just as angry and saw no reason why he should not open his mouth as wide as Gil Delgado.

"What rights have we then?" he shouted.

"You know very well," replied the little crook in collar and tie with all the courtesy of his dirty trade. "You have the right to elect your government, to a minimum wage and to support in time of unemployment. The State is your father. We are no longer in the old days when the Company could ship out its men to starve."

"But to how much liberty have we a right?"

It appeared that they had a right to all the liberties of a good citizen, and the man from the Union had made another fine speech, asking for his name and addressing

himself to Don Rafael, though what in the name of God he
had really said no one could remember afterwards. So the
men elected a committee and chose Gil and Rafael to
negotiate for them. Not because they were experienced.
Just because they were the two who had spoken out.

He and Gil were treated very smoothly as if they were
men of consequence, and they were not suspicious. There
were telegrams and telegrams and then the Ministry proposed that the four hundred and seventy should go to the
Capital in the Company's launches and see for themselves
what was offered — the conditions of work, the wages, the
housing.

The men agreed at once. Were they not human? A little
travel at no expense with wives and children left behind at
Cabo Desierto. Of course they agreed! And the Company
promised to bring back any who were not contented. No
shadow of doubt about it!

"You are trembling," the boy said. "Why?"

"Nothing! Nothing!" Rafael answered, his voice un-
steady.

"Have I asked what a man should not?"

"No, no, beloved. I have my thoughts. That is all."

The jobs which were offered were jobs; a man's prefer-
ence was of no importance. The Ministry wished to distrib-
ute their cattle neatly — a herd here and a herd there —
according to whether they were born on the coast or in the
mountains. So the men became excited and insisted on the
promised right to return to Cabo Desierto while they made
up their minds. There in the Capital they had no one to
fight for them and, worse still, no one they could fight.

Either launches were not available or there were papers to sign which were not ready or secretaries at the Ministry were busy. It was then that he, Rafael, began to be angry, for he had given it as his opinion that the Company could be trusted. Not the Ministry, of course. All of them knew that every politician, however sympathetic, was a liar.

The whole field met in the plaza where there was talk of a strike, but the plaza was too small. Crowds were jammed in the side streets yelling that they could not hear the speakers and overturning vehicles in their way. Thereafter they met in the sports ground, marching out in good order from the town, their own town which was like no other town. What was Cabo Desierto but themselves? It was not right to trick fellow citizens into leaving when they did not want to leave.

In old days the Company had been afraid of nothing, neither the State nor its men nor the devil, but now it was flapping like an old hen with a truck at its tail. They had not known it was screeching, too, until they saw sixty armed police disembarking at the port. And this when they had been told that there were no launches available for their comrades!

The Company should have had more sense than those fools in the Capital for whom Cabo Desierto was a home of ogres in a fairy tale. A ledge of criminals, they called it. Was a decent citizen a criminal just because there was no road or railway to his town? And what was the use of sixty policemen among fifteen hundred oil workers with their knives and spanners?

Well, it had been very plain to the police that they

should keep out of the dispute as best they could. A little blood in the gutters, yes, but thank God no one had been killed! And after the police had returned to their station in the customs shed Cabo Desierto gave them no more trouble.

So all was quiet. But the riot had frightened some women. Women, when their men are away, will believe anything. God only knew what chitchat went on amongst them. They had no more sense than animals. The group which had caused the trouble were the poorest of all, living in the dirty shacks beyond the port, whose husbands, being unskilled, were among the four hundred and seventy stuck in the Capital. It was incredible what some decent men would marry. Nothing in their heads but bed and chatter! One couldn't say much for priests and their fancy dress, but at least they gave such women some sense.

Yet he had no right to be angry with them just for the sake of Catalina. Men are what they are and women are what they are, and when you know what they are it is criminal to take away their husbands and send for the police. A pitiable panic! And they kept their secret as if they were still living in some trapped tribe. Jesus! Would you believe it? A party, all from one lane behind the refinery, went off by land with their children to join their husbands.

That could be done by men who were strong and well-provided and sure of not losing the track which wound and climbed through sixty waterless miles of giant foothills where wind and the trickling gravel could wipe out all sign of it. But for them, impossible! And it was a day before any sensible Christian knew where and when they had gone.

Another day passed without news, and then the Superintendent himself set out after them with four good fellows and his own wife and Catalina. The women would listen to her, and the doctor told her what to do if they and their children were dying of thirst.

A coward, the General Manager with his telegrams! Nothing but telegrams for the help of the army and a plane. Anyone could have told him that the poor martyrs would hide because they were afraid of being sent back. Meanwhile the Superintendent found them in a rocky cove — seventeen of them dead and the rest giving the children sea water to drink because they cried.

They had no longer the strength to walk. The only way to save them was by sea, and that was almost beyond hope even for the men of the port who could handle a boat in any surf. Somehow they got those helpless women off, but Catalina was drowned and two men pulped on the rocks trying to save her.

Yes, and after that there was a tanker at once to take the four hundred and seventy men back to Cabo Desierto. But not to work! No, friends, not to work! The Union refused to back the boycott. It told the unwanted men that they must go and that then it would get higher wages for the rest. Its leaders were not going to draw on the funds which kept them living in the cafés of the Capital. But workers in the country sent what they could and there were contributions from oil fields in all Latin America. Everyone had to tighten his belt a hole, but not yet two. It was a miracle what Cabo Desierto could achieve when all were working full time on the communal lands.

So much discipline and activity — and still there remained his son's question.

"Look!" Rafael told him. "We are not God Almighty to share out the blame. But the Company killed her, and it is on the Company that we avenge her."

TWO. The office of the Compañía Petrolífera Cabo Desierto in London Wall had served the Company for the thirty-five years of its life and in an old-fashioned way was still luxurious, paneled in light oak, furnished with green leather chairs of great comfort, decently spacious and designed to appeal to the financier or shareholder or fellow oilman who might have, regrettably, to wait. The buying of the Company's stores and the selling of its products was carried on across the river at Bermondsey. There, too, the waiting room had changed little. It was furnished for commerce rather than finance and still uncomfortable.

The sole occupant of the green leather chairs would have suited London Wall or Bermondsey equally well. He might have been a sales manager or geologist back from abroad, spare, tall, in his early fifties, with a face once bronzed but now yellowish from lack of sun and the forgotten illnesses of his youth. It was a classless face, having little in common with the firm mouth and professionally kindly expression of the soldiers and colonial administrators. The gray eyes were indeed kindly, but ironical; they had watched rather than accepted, seen through rather than overseen. An employer — a real intelligent tycoon out of the top drawer — could never be quite sure that such a mouth, disturbingly mobile and compassionate, would not smile at what was serious or let loose in the solidity of the board room the outrageous bitter laughter of its unstable habitation.

Matthew Darlow felt himself out of place in London Wall. Bermondsey was all he expected. Presumably they did not know that he would gladly have taken a job as chief clerk — even as a night watchman if it came to that. When he met Henry Constantinides he had fortunately been a little drunk. Not as in old days! The price of alcohol now limited him to an occasional beer. A few gins and some wine with dinner, which had once been as normal an intake as the bread on his plate, produced in these days a vulgar self-confidence, followed in the loneliness of his bedroom by a depth of melancholy which he had to discipline himself to ignore.

18

Two years before, he could still tell any promising acquaintance what he wanted. Now, however delicately he put his request, it sounded in his own ears as if he had shouted: "For Christ's sake give me a job!" But that genial night in a friend's house had temporarily restored the sense of belonging to his normal world. When Henry Constantinides had asked him what he was doing he answered casually that he had practically retired but might be open to any interesting offer. Henry had looked him over carefully, said little, and asked for his telephone number. Mat Darlow didn't think he had been taken in for a moment. Still, the references for half his life had been demanded and the invitation to call at London Wall had come.

He was used to humbly waiting in offices — a poor end to more than thirty highly enjoyable working years in which he had always served his masters better than himself. The Compañía Petrolífera Cabo Desierto had been his second employer and his first love. For five years his job as Secretary and Assistant to the General Manager had been wholly satisfying. The concentration of human beings where they had no right to be provided his character, even then that of a fascinated observer, with interests which married into his daily work. Texas drillers and the hybrid laborers of the coast equally rejoiced him by their departure from the norms of European behavior. And the Company had been generous with local leave. One could jump on a launch to the Capital for the asking.

Why had he left them? Well, would anyone really want to spend his life between Cabo Desierto and London? That answer was instant, yet followed by sour self-reproach.

Irresponsible! Too many employers just for the sake of curiosity. If only he had stopped then, at the beginning, the exasperating pattern of his life!

But at twenty, thirty, even forty, one could not foresee the need for some sort of security at fifty. Security was like death. Obviously it would happen, and obviously you didn't know how. After Cabo Desierto had come Central America; after that, the Congo. All training for each other. It was odd how Spanish civilization taught a man to be on easy terms with any people of any color. You were conditioned to profound respect for the individual though you might have none at all for his way of life. In the end white men, not black, had tired his taste for Africa; they did not want to understand or they understood too scientifically. It was depressing, when he came to think of it, that he had refused careers from sheer impatience with the stupid, whether they were plain inhuman or, to his mind, over-earnest.

Couldn't the stupidity be his own? Well, he had not shown any in London before the war when he was in business for his own account and using his bit of capital for the import of rare woods. He had acted as his own salesman, traveling with a special van full of his lovely samples from the rain forests — silver and red and black and all the yellows from palest lemon to flame. Inch planks, four feet by two. He usually had to start his sales patter in the general office, but in a few minutes the builders or architects or furniture-makers were out in their yards, fascinated by his polished beauties as he slid them off the racks.

Of course he had not made out of it all that he might have done; but it was an assured living, ready for expansion whenever profits allowed. If the war had not come along, he might have had time to buy a house in the country, look around, and get married.

Marriage and children. Prosperity. Christ and Recristo and Damn and Redamn! Why wreck a solid future, so late begun, by enlisting like a boy of twenty? There was no reason for pride in rising from private to full colonel. Anyway he had enjoyed himself far too much to bother with pride. And such promotion was inevitable for a man of wide experience who could command with confidence the languages and customs of the commanded.

On his return to his own country in 1946 he had caught the general sense of exhaustion in a gray, featureless culture. Even he, who had exploited the world of free enterprise to its farthest limits of freedom, was now wary of it. Besides that, he had new assets — among them a minor decoration and a wry taste for government service. So he had taken a sound, unadventurous job in Timber Control. He congratulated himself on being sensible at last; in a few years he would rank as an established civil servant with a pension when he retired.

Timber Control was abolished too soon for that. He was disappointed but felt no grievance. It was high time for an end to import licenses together with the administrators who grew fat on them. He was assured that with his experience he wouldn't have any trouble in getting a business job. Not the slightest, old boy! Did they know that was nonsense or — cushioned from the crude world — didn't they? He never could decide.

Suddenly he was conscious that he, who in his own mind had stayed permanently in the late thirties, was now fifty-two. Responsible posts were no longer for him. He didn't fit into the pension schemes. He had, officially, only thirteen years of useful work left — though that was time enough, one would have thought, to ensure the success of any small firm bumbling along without any original mind at the top. But how to prove the original mind? Employers very naturally thought there must be something wrong with a man of fifty-two who was on the market. The Welfare State would not of course let him starve. His local Labor Exchange had even offered to have him trained for rug-making.

"Sir Dave Gunner and Mr. Constantinides will see you now, Colonel Darlow."

He resisted the impulse to correct the little honey. Inwardly and outwardly he had become Mr. Darlow within three weeks of demobilization. No doubt these people in the outer office were carefully instructed to hand out any title which could conceivably flatter vanity — their own or the caller's.

Henry Constantinides, leaning against the broad, carved mantelpiece of the board room, looked very much the gray-streaked, genial Managing Director. He was still recognizable as the young financier, daring and highly intelligent, who in 1930 had spent a month at Cabo Desierto trying to pick the brains of the General Manager and the Fields Manager. The General Manager hadn't any and the conversational powers of the Fields Manager, who had, were limited to smut. They had used young Mat Darlow as their interpreter, and it had been he who initiated Constantinides into the dynamism of a new and appallingly speculative field.

Yes, Henry was still the same: a real professional City gent, expensively educated, with one generation of money behind him — how it had been made Lord knew — and some little adventurous Greek of a type which Mat had always relished. Their lives were more rootless than his own, yet they made money.

"Ah, Mat!" Constantinides greeted him as if he were a delightful and quite unexpected visitor. "This is Sir Dave Gunner, our Chairman."

Sir Dave had no affectations, except to dress deliberately as if he had just bought his suit off a hanger in a back street of Leeds. He spoke with a firm Yorkshire accent and shook hands as if he had learned the true grip by correspondence course — all qualities which befitted an honest broker between Capital and Labor.

Mat Darlow knew all about Sir Dave — once secretary of a vital trades union, now retired and collecting directorships. One couldn't call him a fraud. Far from it. He had fully deserved his knighthood if he wanted one. No, it was simply that this born negotiator (didn't they call him?) could not be imagined as doing much more than negotiate. Henry, on the other hand, was an honest, aggressive manipulator of money. Instead of peddling paraffin, buttons and rubber goods, as his father might have done, he peddled the companies which manufactured them.

Sir Dave plunged into the interview with a proper north-country objection to wasting time.

"Now, what has been your attitude to Labor?" he asked.

"I don't have one," Mat answered. "I have never been able to see where Labor begins and ends."

"Labor is what gets paid every week," Henry said.

"When it gets paid at the end of the month, it isn't Labor."

A useful definition for practical purposes. That brisk mind could always be trusted to oversimplify anything. Sir Dave did not comment, but added in the tone of an evangelist:

"Labor, Colonel Darlow, responds to leadership. Leadership in the Trades Unions. Leadership in our great firms which are the envy of the world. Labor cannot think for itself. It requires leadership."

True enough, but misleading as talking of a nation as "she." How the devil could any sensitive man, with his mass memories of cheerful faces and easygoing characters, lump together those individuals as "it."

"Sir Dave has faith in generals," Henry said. "But I have managed to persuade him that heartiness of manner might not be enough for Cabo Desierto."

"Trouble with the men?"

"We had to lay off some eight hundred and seventy when the third of the Sentinels came in. The Three Sentinels. Because the rigs were on the skyline of the first ridge. Sounds more imposing than 97, 98 and 98A, doesn't it?"

Mat agreed, and there was silence. Apparently the Board wanted his advice or the use of his memory; but Henry, for an incisive man, seemed reluctant to come to the point.

"You knew in your time that there was oil at thirteen thousand feet," said Sir Dave.

His remark was almost an accusation, as if the pioneers of thirty years earlier must take part of the blame for whatever was wrong.

"The geologists always thought it likely. We used to wonder if it would ever be possible to drill to that depth."

"It was not till 1950 — not for a company of our re-sources at any rate," Henry said. "Up to then the field had stayed as you remember it — bailing and pumping wells working at under two thousand feet. They brought in No. 97 in 1954 and had the fright of their lives before they could cap it. Then 98 and 98A came in this year.

"So we closed down the shallow field. There's oil in it still, but why pump when we can fill the tanks by turning a cock? That meant we had surplus labor. Some of them refused to go."

"But they couldn't stay with no wages."

"We'd made it a home from home for them, see?" said Sir Dave. "A bloody garden city with clubs, canteens, allotments, the whole bag of tricks except a Women's Institute."

"They insisted they could live off the land," Henry explained. "Growing maize on the sports ground, our Gen-eral Manager called it. He turned it down flat. Myself, I wanted to hear more details."

"We could not allow a slum to grow up," Sir Dave rebuked him. "So the Company very generously shipped them off to inspect the jobs which were waiting for them, and Birenfield, our Manager, arranged that they should have plenty of time to make up their minds. But no patience! No gratitude at all! And then a foolish party tried to join them on foot."

On foot! The overland track had been used solely and very rarely by such tough, undesirable characters as could not establish a right to passage in the launches. Henry's father — the father, that is, whom he had invented for

25

Henry — would have been just the fellow to go by land with a load of contraband on his back or his mule.

"Why weren't they sent by launch?"

"They left without saying anything. It's believed they were frightened when the police arrived. There was some street fighting."

"Afraid of the police? In my time, if there was real trouble threatening, we used to give the police a day off to go fishing."

Sir Dave stared at him. He remarked that Colonel Darlow's comment was just the sort of shrewd advice the Company needed and that, aye, he might do.

"You want me at Cabo Desierto?"

"As temporary General Manager," Henry said.

It was desperately disappointing. Henry must have forgotten that he had never been an oil engineer.

"You have taken up my references?"

"All of 'em," Sir Dave answered aggressively. "And I tell you straight that if we could find an experienced oilman with the qualities we want, I'd snap him up. But what with all these new fields in Canada and Arabia there aren't enough good men to go round. So the next best thing is a chap who knows the place and has proved he can manage native labor even if he's not so young as he was. What we want you to do is to break the strike, stay on a bit, and then hand over."

"What's the real grievance? Just the dismissals?"

"They claim that some women died."

"Seventeen women and five children died on the overland track and two men and one woman trying to rescue them," said Henry Constantinides with a clarity which was openly contemptuous of his Chairman. "Now you know what you are up against."

"What do they propose?"

"Nothing! That's the damnable part of it. Their attitude is: You broke a promise, you killed our women, you shall have no more oil ever. And they mean the blasted republic quite as much as us. The Ministry sent the police. We didn't."

"With the full approval of the Miner's Union," Sir Dave added. "And I want you to remember, Colonel Darlow, that the strength of the Union must be built up. Organized Labor is the only hope of stability in these backward countries where governments change once a month."

"Sir Dave has a point there," Henry said. "But unfortunately they threw the Union delegates into the sea."

He did not sound as if he thought it unfortunate. Mat at once tried to divert an argument which could end with both men putting the blame for it on him.

"Has there been any Communist influence?" he asked.

"Of course!" Sir Dave bubbled. "They are largely responsible."

Henry's silky voice murmured that, to those less familiar with the international labor movement, evidence was lacking.

"That is not at all what I hear from private sources," said Sir Dave, ignoring his Managing Director and turning to Mat. "But the Union assures me that they know how to deal with this wildcat strike if we turn a blind eye, give 'em a free hand and afterwards increase the pay packet."

Mat smiled politely and remarked that in his time the

field was always on the boil but on the whole a happy family.

"Which is why I want you," Henry replied. "Can you recover that feeling?"

"I can try. But your present General Manager?"

"Birenfield lost his nerve. Or his wife did. Resigned and cleared out."

"Who's in command at the moment?"

"Gateson, the Field Manager. Afraid of nothing when it's a technical question, but no knack of handling men."

"Birenfield and Gateson were on the right track," Sir Dave insisted. "The men are only foreigners. Some of 'em as black as my hat! On the other hand, Colonel Darlow, a Company which is a model employer with — ah — prominent figures on its Board cannot risk open bloodshed and unfavorable publicity."

Steady now! When the Chairman of the Compañía Petrolífera Cabo Desierto had been inspired by heaven and Henry Constantinides to drop the end of all misery into one's lap it wouldn't do to tell him that he stank. And, anyway, not a quarter of the story had come out yet. The Company, too, had a case. It was exasperating to have so housed and contented your men that they refused to leave.

"What would the Board offer?"

"Ten thousand and a year's contract."

"Anything afterwards?"

"A directorship," said Sir Dave, "would not be beyond the bounds of possibility."

Lord, and half an hour before he could only remember that he was an unwanted fifty-two and that anyone could see his suit was old.

"I'd prefer it to be well within them."

"Frankly I doubt if it would be," Henry said, again cutting through Dave Gunner's evasions. "You're not a businessman, Mat. You never were. Don't regret it! You've had a lot of fun by not being. Take your ten thousand and another ten — the accountants can cook it to be tax free — if you set the oil flowing and don't get us in Dutch with the Government! Your lawyer and ours will have to put that into some sort of form, but we both know what I mean."

"When do you want me to leave?"

"Early next week if you can. Fly to Barranquilla and then on down the coast. You've no attachments?"

None. For the past two years he had bitterly congratulated himself that there were none. But now the implication of that kindly inquiry shattered the unison of his personal flourish of trumpets. Good God, he couldn't even produce an illegitimate daughter, say, to whom half his salary should be paid! His life had been rich in meetings and partings and good fellowship; but all the scattered men and women for whom he had deep affection, probably returned, seemed at any given moment to be absent in time or place.

"No," he answered casually, "no attachments."

THREE. It was in a sense a homecoming, though Mat was far from feeling any spiritual honeysuckle round the door. The first sight of Cabo Desierto was more like the dream of early youth, familiar surely to every man, in which he finds himself, with all his adult experience, confusedly doing his best at school or in his first job. The haze of sun and friendliness, of romance and ambition which had once transfigured for him that prehistorically arid coast had vanished; but the plain facts stood firm and were unexpectedly familiar.

"It hasn't much changed," he said.

The master of the Company's launch, standing formally at the wheel since he was about to enter the Company's port, looked down from the grating almost with tenderness. He claimed to have known Mr. Darlow twenty-five years before. It was likely. Mat had no idea which of the band of black, brown or whitish children this sympathetic seaman had been, but it was easy to pretend a solid image within the cloud of so many common memories.

"It is we who have changed," the skipper replied.

That elegiac note sounding all the way from Spain. How they loved, these Latin Americans, a resounding commonplace! And always it made speaker and hearer conscious of their bond of humanity.

No, Cabo Desierto had not changed — lost its untidy air of pioneering, of course, and lost its youth in the process like the rest of them. The forest of derricks, bailing and pumping away on the second ridge of the hills so that one could hear the thudding of beams and engines two miles offshore, was now silent and looked vaguely derelict, outmoded as a cluster of windmills with all its timber food for the termites. Between the sea and the escarpment of the first ridge, where in early days had been waterless desert, twelve hundred acres of cultivated land extended northwards. The green ribbon tying up such overpowering, colorless immensity emphasized more than ever the islanded quality of the place.

He was glad that he was coming in by sea. The Company's managerial plane had been at the airport on his arrival in the Capital. At the end of a day of champagne, offices and futility, the Ministry had advised him not to take it. Accidents, they whispered, could so easily be arranged. He didn't believe it, and would have taken the plane as a first profession of faith if the unsuspecting pilot had not vanished into the mountains with a girl. Good luck to him! The right way to enter Cabo Desierto was the public way — swept in by the unperturbed Pacific, not descending from heaven to a sacred airfield like a London Wall Elijah.

The launch entered the gateway of brown stone and creaming backwash. Two breakwaters there were now. A tanker could suck up her cargo in any weather. What an amazing place it was, with no economic need of road or railway! A prison, yes, but their isolation, their excited hunting and spearing of the hills used to produce such comradeship between oil engineers and their gunbearers that when the gas and black blood gushed from a lucky stab of the earth they had been as close in triumph as a band of pygmies inside an elephant.

To what had they been loyal in all that orgy? To the Company? To the exploration itself? Most probably to the easily visible achievement. Whatever it was, the solidarity still held, though now it was not directed towards anything; it was directed against — against the Company.

"Remember you are back at home, Don Mateo!" said the skipper.

That word of hospitable encouragement was just what he needed, and the Spanish form of his name gave him an unaccountable lift of morale. Mat Darlow was a failure and employed on a job that no one else would look at; but Don

Mateo was a free man whose power to take action was scarcely limited by London and not at all by Cabo Desierto.

The inshore end of the breakwater was crowded with idle workers, some unashamedly curious, some pretending to be fishing. Mat met their eyes impassively and instantly asked himself what the hell Don Mateo thought he was about. He raised his somewhat theatrical Panama hat in a genial salute and wished them a very good afternoon.

At the landing stage the faces had a standardized smile on them, welcoming but decently conscious of emergency — a string of masks which in a week's time would have sorted themselves out into lively features of friends and enemies. On the quay a separate group, loitering with detached insolence, looked like the boycott committee. Was his reception to be unpleasant? But of course not! Hostility was seldom an excuse for bad manners. It was macabre to the English way of thinking that a man should be capable of apologizing to you before cutting your throat, yet the gesture did add a gentlemanly ease to the proceedings.

He climbed the steps and shook hands with the chief executives of the Company. Then Gateson, the Field Manager, properly observing protocol, introduced the Mayor, the captain of police, the harbormaster and minor civil authorities. Mat had not expected to see behind the port a street of shops shaded by a colonnade with a public building at the far end of it; in his day there had been a sandy road between shacks of timber. The removal of citizens from — well, one could now call it a town — was not so reasonable as it had seemed in London. On an impulse he said he would like to greet the men's leaders if they were

33

present. Those introductions too, went smoothly except, he observed, for the Field Manager. His spirits rose. He wasn't doing too badly for an old horse of no value to anyone but the knackers.

His own car and chauffeur waited on the quay. The glossy length was incongruous when the farthest possible drive was not more than seven miles; they used to lurch around Cabo Desierto in anything which had four wheels and the strength to carry a load. Gateson got in with him, and they drove up the sweeping hairpins of the road to the top of the first ridge, three hundred feet above the sea. Away to the right, above the tank farm on one side and a golf course on the other, were the three concrete sheds of 97, 98 and 98A. Low, square and uncompromising, they looked like pillboxes commanding the harbor.

"Before I meet anyone else," Mat said, "introduce me to the Three Sentinels."

"The bastards won't let you near them."

"One can but try. And they'll enjoy a chance to look me over. Why are they guarding them?"

"They think that between us we could fill a tanker. How the hell are we going to when they control the port?"

The car stopped short of 97. There were half a dozen toughs outside the pillbox. Three of them continued to play cards with an indifference that was deliberately contemptuous. The other three lounged over to the car and ordered the driver to turn round and clear out. Arms were apparently in short supply. The leader had drawn a well-oiled, first-war bayonet from its sheath. The rest had only machetes and steel bars.

Mat's swift first impression was that the power behind

34

the boycott was moral rather than material and thus all the more formidable. Obviously this picket could not stand against determined attack by the police or the military, but any attempt to dislodge it would be the signal for all Cabo Desierto to erupt. The determination up there echoed the calm confidence of the leaders who had shaken hands with him. The Company, they knew, was helpless. As for the State, it could not regain control without adding another pile of corpses to those of eighteen women, five children and two men. The politicians in the Capital had made it very clear to him that they were too humane for that — or too afraid. Under all their noble eloquence he had detected an uncertainty whether the troops would in fact obey the order to fire.

Mat left the car and exchanged normal politenesses with the three guards who confronted him.

"And good evening to you, Mr. Manager! What is it that you want?"

"Only to say good evening also to the Sentinel since I have come all the way from London to see him."

"He is the same as any other."

"You think so? But neither you nor I are the same as any other."

That at least got him a smile. The leader could not as yet replace his bayonet in its sheath but at least he laid it across his other arm.

"And you can see that I come to pay my respects with not so much as a spanner or a screwdriver. In this heat one is barely decent."

His white suit was all dark and transparent with sweat. He was aware that it was due to the last hour of tension as much as to long absence from the fury of the sun, and hoped that no one else could suspect it.

"Give me your matches and cigarettes!"

Mat handed them over and was escorted into 97 by the whole guard, curious to see the two powers confront each other.

Inside its housing of heavy, removable, concrete panels the Christmas Tree emerged from the temporary floor of planks which had been fitted over the well cellar. Its name was apt, for the branching pipes were decorated by starlike wheels controlling the valves; however, the only tree to which it had any resemblance was a mangrove, since the steel branches themselves sprouted shoots upwards and downwards. The pattern of quadrilaterals repressed and channeled the pressure of the advancing Andes upon the oil sands thirteen thousand feet below.

Recovering matches and cigarettes, he returned to the car and a Gateson whose face was white and set with anger.

"The bloody ignorant fools! They're terrified even with all chokes shut down. They could light a bonfire round it so long as they didn't cut the tubing. And if they did, I'd have it under control a couple of hours after they ran away — those of them who weren't cooked or gassed on the spot."

"Ah, but No Smoking sounded efficient, you see. Now, tell me — suppose you let a monkey loose in there to twiddle any valves he liked, a monkey with my box of matches?"

"He couldn't do much harm — at least nothing spectacular," Gateson replied. "But if he twiddled at random and then went down to the casinghead gasoline plant with your matches, we'd need a new plant."

36

"And a new monkey?"

"Quite certainly."

"Perhaps that's what they were thinking of."

"They don't know any more than . . ."

Mat mentally finished the sentence for him. Than you, he was going to say. Lord love a duck, a nasty temper and jealous too! Mr. Gateson's specialty was evidently minerals rather than men.

"What were you producing up to the boycott?"

"Nearly a thousand tons a day from 97 and 98; 98A was closed down as soon as we brought it in. From all three we could do six thousand tons a day and go on for a generation, but what's the use till London has solved the marketing problems?"

Good God, and only eighteen months ago it had been just a hobby for a financier like Henry Constantinides — an innocent little field selling the produce of its shallow wells up and down the Pacific coast as easily as coal, cement or any other bulk commodity! Cabo Desierto was not prepared for the gargantuan vomitings of the Three Sentinels with only a twopenny refinery, two good old tankers and one new. Henry's intention was to sell the whole damned field to one of the major oil companies which could afford to keep it on the ice till it was needed. But just what was its value so long as the boycott lasted?

They drove down the shallow valley between the first and second ridges where the barren gravel had been redeemed from original sin by the bungalows, lawns and messes of the executive staff, all angelically set among the flowers and giant shrubs of an equatorial coast. At the end of the avenue of neat Company palms a road ran halfway

37

up the second ridge to the General Manager's house. Mat's impression was one of magnificent emptiness. That was because the house stood alone in the middle of a terraced garden with windows looking west to the arc of the Pacific and south over the roofs and greenery towards the Three Sentinels.

Inside, too, was emptiness. The Company's excellent furniture was formally arranged. The Company's house-man greeted him with exactly the right degree of respectful cordiality. But there was no sign, not even a dirty ashtray, of the last or any occupants. The swept house emphasized his loneliness. Nothing belonged to him but the two suit-cases which the houseman had just placed in his bedroom. If only one of the cases had been a woman's, she'd have made enough mess in five minutes to create the appearance of a home.

"Don't go yet," he said to Gateson. "Stick around while I change if you're not too thirsty!"

"Pepe can deal with that," the Field Manager replied. "We put enough stores in the cellar to carry you through for a week or two."

Who were "we," he wondered with a sudden collapse of self-confidence, and what had been the anxious, half-patronizing gossip before his arrival? But Pepe, white-jacketed, was already hovering over the cocktail cabinet. Luxury in this loneliness at any rate. The energy of the General Manager was not to be expended in the handling of drinks himself.

"A long whisky please, Pepe," Gateson said.

"I'll have a quick shower and then join you."

When he had returned to the living room and downed

the first tall glass of the tropical evening he felt the Darlow of ten years earlier. It was absurd to blame his temporary home for emptiness when from a window you could see or think you saw the curve of the globe.

"My wife and I hoped you would dine with us. We'll just have a few people in afterwards and an early night. You must be tired."

Nothing for it but to accept gratefully. Well-spaced alcohol would see him through.

"And one other thing — I've arranged a police guard after what happened."

Mat was not going to admit that there was something the Board had not chosen to tell him. He had put down the sudden resignation of his predecessor to nervous exhaustion and had never asked any direct question about his private reasons.

"I know the facts, of course," he said cautiously, "but not the details."

"There aren't any. He was shot at twice sitting in the window where I am now."

"Kind of you."

"Oh, they wouldn't risk it again. There's a machine gun covering the gate."

"Will it fire?"

"I suppose so."

"Then I'll have it removed. Machine guns demoralize me when I can't see where they are pointing. What happened after they missed him?"

It was a fair bet that they had. Henry and Sir Dave would have been in honor bound to mention it if the General Manager had been wounded. But if there had merely been some irresponsible shooting — or what they could reasonably consider as such — why be alarmist?

"His wife, I am afraid, insisted that he should go."

"Anything in particular which upset the field?"

"It's said it was because he offered compensation to the men who had lost their families."

"Sorry your missus was such a damn fool as to get killed. Here's fifty quid to buy yourself another."

"While emphasizing that the Company accepted no legal obligation," added Gateson, staring at him.

"Now, tell me — I see domestic staff is not on strike. What's the position?"

"The men refuse us any oil except to the power station. Otherwise life is normal."

"And who knows everybody's names and faces?"

"Ray Thorpe, the Superintendent."

Mat asked what sort of man he was, remembering that he had led the rescue party.

"Inclined to have a foot in both camps — not what one would expect from a chap who won a Military Cross in the D-day landings. Had the luck to be seen, I suppose."

Yes, and probably the first person to admit it. Evidently Thorpe was the man whose confidence must be won, on whose view of the situation a temporary opinion might be based until he had one of his own.

Mat went off to Gateson's damned dinner — unfair, that! Kind and very correct dinner — looking forward to Thorpe who wasn't there. He sensed that the guests had been chosen from the Gatesons' intimate friends of their own upper middle class background, not wholly according to rank in the Company. Dangerous self-confidence, if so.

There were half a dozen couples in all, the odd woman being his own private secretary, Pilar Alvarez, who came of an old and aristocratic family and looked it.

Mrs. Gateson was delightfully hospitable and hard as nails — more like a practiced army wife, he thought, than an oil wife. She talked London. She knew the Gunners and was cautiously amusing at their expense. Then she brought up the nervous Mrs. Birenfield who had been such a dear, close friend. Mat was aware of being summed up as a possible collaborator.

"What did you think of your chauffeur?" she asked.

It was a curious question. He couldn't have any worthwhile impression as yet. He had only shaken Lorenzo's hand and passed a few cordial remarks. His driver was a pure Indian of the round-headed, rather Mongolian type, as imposingly correct as a hired butler and a lot more silent. At a guess, he was not intelligent; on the other hand, judging by his appearance and that of the managerial car, he was very conscientious.

"Makes me feel like a millionaire," Mat said.

She let that go, revealing nothing of her own opinion if she had one, and turned him over to Pilar Alvarez — charming, efficient and perhaps a Ministry spy. But never mind that! He was glad she was a woman of the country, not a machine import.

With the coffee the rush started. Faces, faces. Shaking hands and trying to say the right thing — a different right thing — to everybody. After an hour of it he was let off, to be driven home by Lorenzo. The man could be talked at for a year and still leave little impression. Yet Mrs. Gateson must have had some reason for mentioning him. She was a much cleverer person than her husband.

The police post at his gate at least showed its presence and saluted. There was no sign of the machine gun. It was probably sited behind a low wall from which an appetizing smell of fish stew was wafted into the car. A typically bloody fool place commanding only the approach to the house. Anyone who chose to crawl down from the hillside and into the cover of a higher terrace could — if merciful — plug one neat shot into the stew pot and the fight would be over.

Pepe hovered hospitably. His wife Amelia — and Don Mateo's cook, very much at his service — would like to know what he preferred for breakfast. Coffee, he replied, and fresh rolls and — could there be a papaya in the larder? Pepe did not know but pronounced that there would certainly be iced papaya on the table at eight A.M. Through the weary years of London, papaya had become a symbol of sun and birds and the fresh heat of morning. It gave him immense pleasure that there would be papaya. The General Manager admitted that Mat had never quite grown up.

He did not go to bed, knowing that sleep would be impossible until his brain began to drift away from the problems of this community which depended on him. With all lights out, he rested in a deck chair on the veranda, enfolded by the soft darkness in which so many of his nights had been passed, the benevolent successor of the heat. Dream and daydream became hardly distinguishable. Closed eyes or open eyes, one was back — didn't they say? — in the womb. And a damned nice place it would be, too, very like a moonless tropic night with stars — the stars that were to be — covered by sea mist or monsoon cloud.

The silence was absolute. The first ridge cut off the sound of the surf and such night noises as there might be in the town — a traditional little town, not at all badly done by architects who stuck to the old ways. Dave Gunner's home from home. Wonder what he would make of it, especially if a cockroach dropped down his collar from the roof of the colonnade. Probably he'd have the whole place replanned in little boxes to save such a humiliation for Labor.

Yes, there was that noise again. A faint, neat plop. There must have been an earlier, half-noticed pop which put the image of Sir Dave into his head. Rats? Lizards? But they scuttered; they didn't plop. Scorpions? Well, you might get one falling off the terrace, but not a procession. Seagull roosting? Could be, but it must be pretty constipated. Plop!

He got up very quietly and looked over the rail of the veranda at the dark masses of the unfamiliar garden. Again he heard the sound and saw dimly a little spurt of silver. So one of the small, open places was a pool. Fish jumping for mosquitoes? But wrong noise. Fish splashed.

He crossed the stretch of lawn below the house with a caution which seemed absurd when he was merely satisfying curiosity. Whatever the alarmists thought, he was sure there would be no attempt to intimidate him while the field was still doubtful of his character and intentions. Still, it was always wiser to see without being seen.

At the edge of the pool a small boy lay on his belly with

a hand in the water, utterly absorbed. He quickly withdrew his hand, examined the fish he had caught and tossed it back. Mat crept on till there was only a large fern between him and the boy's heels. He tried to remember the Spanish for "tickling trout" and came to the conclusion that he had never known. Not that these were trout. They were some globular and decorative little fish. Fascinated, he continued to watch, then stepped accidentally on a loose stone and showed himself at once.

"Don't be afraid!" he said. "It doesn't matter so long as you put them back."

The child jumped to his feet, standing still as a boy of bronze at the edge of the pool. Defiant, too, as any little animal which hadn't a chance of escape and knew it. His hand clutched the pocket of his dirty trousers.

"It wouldn't stay alive in your pocket," Mat said.

But perhaps he was hungry. No, that wouldn't do. The fish looked inedible; and anyway he had been catching them and throwing them back.

"Do you come here often?"

"No."

"Just to play with the fish?"

"I was waiting," the boy replied indignantly, as if play were quite out of the question.

"For whom?"

"No one."

Odd! He looked as guilty as if he had just walked off with all the silver. Waiting for an accomplice, perhaps. Small boys were often used for unlawful entry.

"Listen, little friend! Let me see what you have there!"

The boy, too proud to be searched, pulled out a stick of

44

toffee wrapped in greaseproof paper. Mat took it from him. Toffee be damned! It was a half-pound stick of gelignite.

He ran his hands over the two cotton garments and discovered nothing else but a box of matches. Inexplicable! Who the devil would send a child out with half a pound of explosives and matches — in the same pocket, too? Answer: nobody. It was the little monkey's own plan, own mischief.

"Why are you carrying this about with you?"

"Because I am a man."

"That can be seen," Mat replied courteously. "But what were you waiting for?"

"I saw the fish on my way."

Very natural to be distracted by fish in a pool at seven or eight or whatever he was.

"On your way to where?"

"To you."

Desperation. Enmity. What stuff to find in this innocent, sharp voice! Nothing made sense. But, yes, it did! Thought a bomb was like a firework. He was going to light his stick and throw it.

"You would just have burned yourself horribly. It wouldn't have gone off."

"Why not?"

"I will show you. Then you can blow me up better next time."

"You are not calling for the police?"

"There is no need for police between *valientes*."

"That is what my father says."

"Who is your father?"

"Rafael Garay."

The blackish leader of the boycott with whom he had shaken hands that very evening. The name had stuck in memory, for he had read it in reports at the London office and heard it again at the Ministry. The man and his dead wife both seemed to be remarkable characters.

"What's he going to say about this?"

Silence.

"You thought he would be pleased?"

"That has nothing to do with you."

"No. No, it hasn't, son. You are right."

It passed through his mind that Rafael Garay could have sent the boy. But that was unthinkable. The little idiot had stolen his stick of gelignite somewhere and set off on his heroic adventure with ridiculous ideas of his own on how it should be used.

"You must wash your hands at once," he said. "Then you can stick your finger up your nose."

"I did not!"

"It's of no importance. There are grown men who do it."

"My mother said there are not."

No arguing with that! Mother's word was considered as coming down from Sinai.

"At Cabo Desierto there are not. But in Europe there are very respectable men who rabbit around in their noses."

"It is a dirty habit," the boy quoted solemnly.

"You are right. It is a dirty habit."

"I do it when I think."

"Come and wash your hands quickly and your nose too! If you don't, that stuff could give you an awful headache."

He put a light hand on the boy's arm so that he could

46

not run away and led him to the bathroom, motioning to him to be quiet. Taps and shower and steaming water made the small amateur assassin very tense — like a man entering some sinister, ultramodern surgery, Mat supposed. But he obediently washed hands and nostrils.

"And now are you ready for the lesson?" Mat asked, leading him back to the garden.

"It is enough."

"Don't you want to learn how to make a bang safely?"

"No, I don't want to. I know what lesson you are going to teach me."

It seemed unnatural for a boy to refuse and to be so frightened. One must use a bit of imagination and put oneself in his place. Man from the moon. Out of another world. Why didn't you beat him up or send for the police? Got it! Because you're going to teach him a lesson yourself. Throw a bomb at me, would you? Right! So we'll see how you like it when that stick is under your backside.

"You think I'm going to blow you to blazes, son? Have some sense and remember I too was a child!"

"True?" he asked with as much amazement as if the General Manager claimed to have been born from a boiled egg.

"True as I stand here. And also I did not have a mother very long."

"Did you have a father like mine?"

"It could be. Yes."

He was surprised by his own sincere answer. What the hell was there in common between a militant black carpenter at Cabo Desierto and an earnest, kindly Fabian in Hampstead who wouldn't hurt a fly? Perhaps Rafael Garay also walked over hills with his son and talked to him as if he were an equal.

"Why did the Company kill my mother?"

"I have heard that your mother gave her life for other women."

"My father says it was the Company."

"That is a manner of speaking. If you had killed me, it could be said that the Company did."

"I do not understand."

"The Company made your father angry. Your father made you angry. So you took vengeance on me. So it is the fault of the Company which sent me here."

"Then everything is the fault of the whole world."

"Very true."

"But my mother is dead!"

This was utterly unexpected. He had an overstrained, weeping child on his hands instead of a desperado. Only one thing to do. Who was it said that the young of every mammal, due to a common softness of face, signaled for help to every other mammal? Probably got it wrong somewhere. Certainly not true for hyenas and lambs. Well, an arm round his shoulders seemed to work here. Poor little blighter! Rafael Garay was a lucky devil. And the boy had such command over his own terrified spirit, both while crawling through the darkness and when caught by this foreigner with an infinite power for evil.

"What time do you go to bed?"

"When I like."

"So your father will say nothing?"

"He will ask where I have been."

"Well, you must never tell him a lie. Say that you came

48

up here to have a look at me and stopped to play with the fish, which is true. Go away as you came and not past the police at the gate! Until we see each other again, and with God!"

The child slipped instantly into the night. Nobody could vanish quicker than a small boy who had been unexpectedly let off, and quite right, too. Get the hell out before the boss changes his mind! Mat strolled back to the pool and buried the stick of jelly under a damp stone. Then he had a go at the fish himself. Couldn't catch one! Cunning little hands were much nearer to nature than General Manager's.

The comic, complex encounter was unexpectedly restful. He slept well. Papaya was up to the highest remembered standard, the question of lunch confidently left to Amelia. Lorenzo, preserving his sergeant-on-parade solemnity drove him down to his office. Cartoon of a capitalist. He only needed a top hat and a cigar.

He was greeted by Pilar Alvarez and decided that in the office she looked as a private secretary ought to look — statuesque, well-groomed, with fine, brown eyes. At a guess, she modeled herself on, say, a minor New York executive, but her warmth was not so standardized. She showed him the files and explained existing routine. After half an hour of it he asked half-humorously:

"Whose side are you on?"

"I am paid to be on yours, Mr. Darlow," she answered as if he had accused her of disloyalty.

A silly, impulsive question it had been. What the devil had he expected her to say? He should have waited a whole intimate office week before probing.

"My shorthand conversation. You'll soon get used to reading it. What I meant was: do you see any solution that we foreigners don't?"

"At present only force."

"Colonels required?"

"They are all glad you were one yourself."

She said "they" not "we," so after all she did not wholly identify herself with the Company. It would be interesting to know why not. Pride perhaps.

"What do you think Mr. Thorpe would be doing now?"

"His inventory, probably."

"Good Lord! Why?"

"None of them like being idle."

"What sort of man is he?"

"Very English."

It was the first unpuzzled smile she had given him. Evidently she liked Thorpe. On the field anything was forgiven to a man of marked character whatever his failings in tact and temperament.

"Could we tell him to drop it and come up here now?"

"We could."

And another of those smiles for himself. But he would have to be careful with her. He sensed a slight contempt for the men, the Company and the whole godawful mess. On the other hand he had no doubt that she could run the correspondence with London and the Ministry nearly on her own, stalling both of them while he got down to essentials.

"See if you can get him, and meanwhile fill up this empty desk with all the stuff I must see and whatever you think I oughtn't to!"

Paper words. Business words. No opinion that was not hedged. There was nothing factual and incisive except from the would-be strong men like Gateson who chose their own facts. He was thankful when Ray Thorpe plunged into the office: short, thick, reliable, intelligent so far as he went. And you will not, he told himself, assume how far he goes. You're the General Manager, not Gypsy Petulengro.

"Tell me what happened. They all talk round it like a cat with a scorpion. How the hell did those women get lost?"

"Well, sir, you don't know the track."

"Yes, I do. Road, rail — we couldn't afford either of them then, but we surveyed routes for the lot before it was decided to stick to water transport."

"They cleared out along the beach at dusk and no one knew a thing till nearly midday. The tide had covered their trail by then."

"Launch?"

"At once. And a land party. But no sign of them by nightfall. They had twenty hours' start. The chaps camped and were up before dawn, sure of finding them for they'd be exhausted after marching at that pace. But still nothing. Half the party with all the water kept up the search. The rest beat it back here."

"What did Birenfield do?"

"Wired for troops, aircraft, the lot. But that took time. At our end he gave up."

"So you went."

"Took a mule pulling fifty gallons of water and our portable wireless. Four of my best men came along and

51

Catalina Garay. The women would listen to her. We knew that."

"And your wife, I hear."

"Had to have another woman."

The brusque reply inhibited any more questions on that subject. But the keep-off sign did not, Mat decided, imply that Mrs. Thorpe had shown any unwillingness. Just the opposite. There was an enviable partnership so intimate that strangers were not admitted.

The women had entered the track all right, but lost their heads when they thought it was leading them too far inland. Their only guide to the Capital was the coast. So they turned off to the south along a tempting bit of plateau — easy walking, Thorpe said, but so hard that a bulldozer wouldn't have left any trace, let alone bare feet. Then they had to march across the lay of the country, up and over bald ridges stripped by trickling gravel and the sun. Up and over. Now waterless and far gone they staggered down to the sea. There was no kindly beach offering a route to the south, only a small cove where the canyon ended at the surf.

"Never saw such a bloody awful place! Yellow death behind you, white death ahead of you. Christ!"

Clinging close to the half-shade of wet rocks, as if they had been the missing husbands damp with loving sweat, the women had properly bitched the searching plane. Bitched the tracked vehicles of the army, too, which dutifully covered impossible valleys. Meanwhile Thorpe's party found them, led by the chance of an empty can shining in the sun. Beyond the next ridge they came on the corpse of a child with a little gravel scratched over it. After that it

was easy for Catalina to guess how the minds of the women
had worked.

There in the cove they were — seventeen of them dead
and the rest giving the children cream of the sea foam
to drink when they cried. Thorpe signaled back his ap-
proximate position and kept a column of smoke going
which was bound to be seen offshore.

"Ourselves, we'd rather have walked back and chanced
it," he said. "But the only hope for the women and children
was the launch."

A boat carrying a line was hurled into the cove at the
cost of one broken arm. The crew rigged a running cable to
the launch, anchored on good ground beyond the surf, and
somehow got those helpless women away. But Catalina was
drowned and lost and two men smashed to pulp trying to
save her.

"And you?"

"Went last. I should have gone first to see how it
worked."

"It wouldn't have done. Sinking ship and all that."

"That's what I thought. But if I'd had real guts I should
have tried it on the dog and let 'em talk afterwards. The
missus would have understood, which is all that matters."

"Who frightened those blasted women out of their wits
in the first place?"

"The Government say Communist agents."

"Under the bed?"

"No. What was on it."

"Facts, please, Mr. Thorpe."

"Can only give you what Catalina told my wife."

"That's probably as near gospel as we're likely to get."

53

"They didn't like their husbands with a pocketful of money among all the dockside whores of the Capital."

"They used to take that as natural — at any rate for a couple of days off. There must have been more to it."

"There was. Police hanging round at night."

"Rape?"

"Worse than that. For money."

"Why weren't they knifed?"

"Nobody knew about it. All the men had gone from those old shacks beyond the refinery."

"But I still don't understand."

"The women wanted to get to their husbands then and there. Not a month or two later, in case of results. I don't mean that they were all at it — only a dozen or so of the dirtiest. But the panic caught on like an epidemic and even the decent ones were infected."

"The women who were rescued — haven't they talked?"

"Not so far as I know. They wouldn't. Their men were shipped back the same week. And my wife and I kept it quiet. We didn't want to be responsible for a massacre."

"You told Birenfield?"

"Yes — when he kept on driveling about left-wing agitators. He didn't believe it. I didn't myself till Jane looked it all up in the library. Collective hysteria, it's called."

"What does the field make of it?"

"Just that. Collective hysteria in their own words. When their husbands were not sent back as promised, the women persuaded themselves they never would be."

"The police must know."

"Those who were responsible, yes. I doubt if Captain Gonzalez does."

54

"We'll leave it that way. Imagine you haven't told me!"

"May I let Jane know that I have?"

Mat noticed the change. First, the facetious "my missus," then "my wife," now "Jane." Confidence was established.

"Of course. Now, when was the last check on the explosives store?"

"Mr. Gateson made one recently, and a police patrol visits the perimeter."

"You mean, it's in their orders to visit."

"Shall we run up there, sir? I have a key."

"Just quietly. In your truck, if it's outside. I don't want to put ideas into anyone's head."

The store was up to professional standard, sheltered by a high earth bank, fenced by unclimbable barbed wire and approached by a narrow road from the abandoned field. The wire was intact and the gate padlocked. Inside the store itself the boxes were neatly stacked, contents labeled, lids sealed. A carbon copy of the inventory was in a frame screwed to the wall. Evidently Gateson had given his personal attention to explosives with model efficiency.

"Just as you remember it, Mr. Thorpe?"

"I think so. You suspect there might be some missing?"

"I only know that they have sticks of gelignite down in the town."

"Then it's not from here. We have no more now — only a little guncotton and some ammonal and dynamite. Personal knowledge, sir, or someone breathing fire over drinks?"

"Personal. Have you ever noticed how the first twelve hours in a new place are often the most productive?"

"I hope to God . . ."

"No. I slept very well."

"To think there was always such goodwill! And now the dead hang over us like those damned hills."

"What would you do in my place to stop them falling?"

"Make a balls of it. I can't bear standing around, so I'd force the pace. Law and order pronto!"

"You think I shouldn't?"

"No. Play it cool and let them come to you."

" 'Rock of Ages' stuff?"

"Eh?"

"Hide myself in thee."

"Well, it looks as if there is room enough," Thorpe replied with a grin.

"Thank you. But the furniture hasn't arrived yet. I have to wander round a bit myself and ask questions."

FOUR.

"Sons," said Captain Gonzalez in a tone that was paternal rather than familiar, "not for a moment do I forget the instructions given to me by the Ministry of Labor in person. Firmness without brutality!"

He did not look paternal, apart from a weariness of expression such as any father might fall back on when exasperated by his own powerlessness. His lemon-colored face was a mask of professional geniality which had long since ceased to reflect moral values.

"It is the duty of all of us," he went on, "to show the world, which has its eyes upon us, that in the Republic the glorious traditions of humanity are preserved."

"Nothing simpler, Captain," Rafael Garay replied, "provided the police keep out of it."

The office of Captain Gonzalez together with barracks for his sixty policemen had been constructed in the Cabo Desierto customs shed. Since the quarters had been furnished by the Company, they were considerably more imposing than the average police station elsewhere. Gonzalez delighted to show himself off in such surroundings and had developed an almost ministerial taste for conferences.

Rafael Garay and Gil Delgado were themselves somewhat impressed by the comfort of the chairs in which they sat opposite the Captain's desk, though they had no respect for the man himself. After the first few interviews with him they had realized that if he were never provoked into leaving his office he was unlikely to do so of his own accord.

"How are your invalids, Captain?" Gil Delgado asked with a faultless pretense of kind inquiry.

"Better. Much better, thank you. What a mercy no one was killed! As it is, I have been able to report that never was the situation out of hand."

That first and decisive battle with the police had been an affair of overwhelming numbers pouring down to the port in a spontaneous burst of anger — a few wild shots on one side, knives and iron bars on the other. Gonzalez, reluctant to admit that his men had run like rabbits, circulated the official myth of a heavily armed gang before which the police had retreated with dignity to avoid provocation and bloodshed. That suited Garay and Delgado very well, for in fact their men had few arms — only a few cheap pistols bought in calmer days more to show to friends than for use, and now some better ones lifted from unconscious policemen. There were not even any sporting guns in a community which had only inedible sea birds to hunt.

"Good, my sons, let us leave it so!" Gonzalez went on. "Least said, soonest mended. But it is my duty to warn you that there must be no interference with that most noble and sympathetic person, our new General Manager. Any accident and you all go to the jail!"

"Who'll take us?" asked Gil Delgado.

"Quietly! Quietly! What can you do against the weapons of the police?"

"Turn them round."

"Gentlemen, I beg of you! Is that the way to talk?" Captain Gonzalez exclaimed, placing his hands upon his desk as if to rise. "All I ask is consideration for Don Mateo."

Truculence, Rafael thought, went down well at meetings but should not become a habit. Gil always liked his power to be felt. There was no object in bullying a man who was always looking over his shoulder in case he got into trouble with the Government or the Company. Gonzalez's dislike of any definite action entirely suited their policy.

"One can always speak with you, Captain," he said, "and be sure of a hearing."

"With you, Sr. Garay, it is always a pleasure. Now, tell me in confidence — has Don Mateo made any offer?"

"There is no offer we will accept."

"Good! I understand your feelings. But if he does, do not take it as an insult!"

"If it is an insult, it is. If it is not, it is not. We want nothing more than to work our lands and forget."

"You are a hard man. In the end you will compel the State to take over the Company."

"If they wish. But they will get no oil."

"You have no duty to the Republic?"

"It had none to us."

"But the work which was offered! There were jobs I should be glad to have myself."

"No doubt they are still available," said Gil Delgado.

Rafael managed to suppress a smile but knew that his eyes had given him away. He often wished that in his interviews with the police and the town worthies he was not escorted by Gil Delgado, although Gil's eloquence and sarcasm were indispensable in committee and at public meetings. He himself — well, what was he? He could only say what he meant simply and honestly. If he was cheered as enthusiastically as Gil, it must be because he was relentless and his comrades knew it.

"Frankly, Sr. Garay, one would expect so sympathetic a man as you to be open to argument," Gonzalez protested.

"Words change nothing, Captain. The State and the Company broke their word and murdered our women."

"You forgive no more than your son."

"My son? What has he to do with it?"

"He told me that when he was big enough he would stick a knife in me."

"You too have children, Captain," Rafael answered hesitantly.

"Yes indeed. And I shall be glad when I can see them again. So it was understood between Chepe and myself that this was to be my fate and that meanwhile, as bitter enemies, he would do me the honor to accept a biscuit."

Gil Delgado remarked that such gentlemanly behavior was out of a romance.

"It seemed to me that for a moment he let me live in one, Sr. Delgado."

Outside the police station a score of men waited idly for the reappearance of their two leaders, enduring the direct blast of the Cabo Desierto sun upon the shadeless concrete of the waterfront. That was the only sign of purpose in the loose gathering which, under its casual cheerfulness, concealed its determination that anyone who entered the station should leave it. Voices became louder and less disciplined when Rafael and Gil walked out on to the quay.

"Nothing in particular," Rafael announced. "Antón!"

A little mestizo, alert as a ferret and wearing the grayish remains of the uniform of some indistinguishable army, answered:

"Chief?"

"Return the police rifle! Throw it through the back window while they are asleep!"

"As you order, Rafael. Is there any danger?"

"None. A favor to Gonzalez — that is all."

There were three cafés under the colonnades of the town. Two were no more than dark taverns. The third, patronized by the Mayor, the harbormaster and the Company's white-collar employees, was on the street level of

61

Cabo Desierto's only hotel and had its waiters, trays and
kitchen staff. Rafael and Gil would never have dreamed of
using it before the boycott, but they were now responsible
citizens. They sat down at one of the dozen iron tables
outside the door and ordered two glasses of the cheapest
rum.

Both were in need of relaxation. There was so much to
do: organization of full-time work on the land, distribution
of relief, posting of guards. On top of all that routine work
was an obstructive bank manager who could not help re-
ceiving the contributions from sympathizers abroad but
made every possible difficulty over the signatures necessary
to draw on them. The last straw was to be compelled to
waste an hour on Gonzalez.

"But there is no point in being rude to him, brother,"
Rafael said.

"What does it matter? He's a coward."

"We do not want them to send the army instead."

"They dare not."

"No, provided we are peaceable. That is what I have
said at every meeting."

"Keep your eyes on me, Rafael! The General Manager
is coming."

"What the devil is he doing out of his car? To me he
seems simpleminded. An unfortunate!"

"Brother, he's going to lose his pants if he doesn't kick
that dog!"

A yellow, short-haired mongrel was excited by the unfamiliar smell of manager. Rafael and Gil leaned forward
delightedly. Mat Darlow, not knowing if the cur belonged
to anyone of importance, was tacking up the street and

avoiding a definite engagement. Aware that in another moment he would become a figure of farce, he decided that the nuisance could no longer be treated as somebody's valued pet. He shot out a hand to his ankles and seized the astonished animal by the scruff of the neck. With his other hand supporting its backside, he lectured it in rich Castilian, finally heaving it gently into the gutter where it, its mother and its daughter had carried on their trade.

The blasted dog was a reminder — not that any was needed — of his isolation. He had been swimming at the country club and had taken a momentary dislike to all the self-satisfied faces. Perhaps it was his age. At any rate he felt himself to be wasting time in a bright half-world which had no more to do with life than a musical film. The background of sparkle and trumpeting flowers and imported palm trees was indeed much the same. So he had driven down to the town and left his car outside the port offices.

Astonishment at seeing the General Manager on foot in the main street was obvious and embarrassing. Very well, let them be astonished! He wasn't manager of anything at all. Managers should have the Company, the Police and the Government behind them. The Company was hoping — with long drinks in the shade — for an energetic offensive. The sole interest of the police was to avoid blame for whatever happened. And the Government, faced by the problem of marketing the bonanza of the Three Sentinels, was not at all eager to take them over and shoot down workers in the name of nationalization.

Wander around a bit and ask questions — he had spent a week on that and received too many answers. The Company executives were sure they had right on their side.

63

Well, from their limited angle so they had. The priest. He couldn't say what Jesus Christ would recommend in a case like this. He was disconcerted by Mat's curiosity. Divinity should stay safely on the Cross. He got more out of Dr. Solano, who at least had shown a professional interest — as if dealing with a cage of rats — in the experiment of living without wages. Undernourishment, he said, was not yet serious and the Cabo Desierto lands could give a poor but adequate standard of living. When he felt free to talk frankly Luis Solano would be an invaluable friend — of far more use than the likable, bumbling Mayor who contradicted himself daily. Before lunch he was horrified at the folly of his fellow citizens; after lunch they had his sympathy.

The police were predictable anyway. They were on the side of religion and property, which was always surprising since they had little of one and none of the other. And that Captain Gonzalez — a timid bureaucrat who seldom dared to show how intelligent he really was! The Manager must not sit in lighted windows. The Manager must not go out alone. Gonzalez would like to see him continually followed by three well-polished, armed half-wits in uniform. That would look well in a report.

No one but he could get Cabo Desierto back to work. No one could help him in more than minor decisions. No one could share his perceptions. But there it was! Without his car and an expression on his face as blank as Lorenzo's he was biteable as any other intruder. The dog was perfectly right. One could only hope that Henry Constantinides was, too.

The café under the hotel was an inviting refuge, though

it was awkward that those two toughs should be sitting there — one black and stocky, the other tall, big-bellied and exceptionally white for Cabo Desierto. Gil Delgado, of course, and Rafael Garay, the father of the boy. However, he had shaken hands with them on arrival, so it would be safe to try a polite bow and sit as far away as possible. Or even join them, damn it! If they were sullen and got up to leave, at least enmity would be clarified.

"With your permission?" he asked, approaching their table.

There were indeed two seconds of hesitation, but due to surprise rather than deliberate coldness.

"Sit down, Mr. Manager," answered Rafael Garay.

Mat drew up a chair, allowed formal courtesies to flower, and was asked what he would take.

"What are you drinking? Rum? That will do me good, too."

"Are you very busy?" asked Gil Delgado when the drink was served.

Mat smiled at the pretended politeness and made a mental note that at some future date the fellow should be pulverized by a sharper irony than his own. He might appreciate it. Reports had it that Garay inspired the troops and the more sophisticated Delgado gave the pep talks.

"Not so busy as I used to be. Here where we are sitting was a quarantine station — nothing but three walls, a thatched roof and a sort of government doctor. I remember he wanted to vaccinate two of our Texas drillers who had just arrived. One of them shot the ampoule out of his hand while the other dealt with the bottles."

"Those were the days!" Gil exclaimed.

"Yes, we wouldn't stand interference from the outside. Did you ever hear that for a week we declared Cabo Desierto an independent republic?"

"Who? The British?" Rafael asked with a shade of resentment.

"Not we! We were sick with laughing. The drilling crews were at the bottom of it. They didn't approve of an import tax on our liquor."

"And was your republic taken seriously?"

"Only by the Government — and the poor harbormaster who had to entertain the ship's company of the gunboat which was sent. Friends, I know we cannot go back to the beginning, but never forget that Cabo Desierto was once my home!"

"It's plain you understand its dogs," said Gil Delgado.

A trap there. If he answered anything like a simple affirmative, the fellow would quote him as saying or implying that the workers of Cabo Desierto were dogs.

"The man who does not understand them is either a fool or a coward. To understand one's fellow citizens is harder. But perhaps we could work together in some things."

"For example?" Rafael asked.

"For example, something healthy to drink while none of us has much money. There is a surplus of wine in Chile. It would be very cheap and the duty is low. Shall I buy in bulk for the canteen?"

"We cannot use the canteen."

"Who is stopping you?"

"Man, it's understood."

"So long as it is not against your principles! In my day it

66

might have been. There was always a taste of oil in everything."

"You would permit it?"

"Why not? The cooks and servers might as well do some work for their pay. And the profit, if there is any, goes to the Welfare Fund."

"We cannot draw on the Welfare Fund."

"But it is yours like the land."

"No! The land belongs to the Cooperative. But the Fund belongs to the employees of the Company. And since we are no longer employees . . ."

"I see. You should be a lawyer, Sr. Garay. But I hear there is some suffering."

"Among the children," Rafael admitted.

"You have a son, I believe. What is his name?"

"Chepe," Rafael answered and then, feeling that the nickname was too informal for managerial society, added: "José-Maria."

"Doña Catalina was a churchwoman?"

"Yes, but she had no need to be."

"I have heard that where she was, was heaven already."

Rafael did not respond. The General Manager had no right to state a truth which had never — in so many words — occurred to him.

"I will see what I can do about the Welfare Fund. Lend it to the Mayor, perhaps. We do not want children in our battle."

"There is no battle, Mr. Manager," Rafael said impassively. "This is a boycott, not a strike."

"What do you propose to end it?"

"Nothing. We of Cabo Desierto have decided to live without oil."

"And what do *you* propose?" Gil asked.

"Also nothing. Since we are agreed, some more rum? And as I am an older inhabitant than either of you I must be permitted to pay."

"We thank you," said Rafael, rising. "But we have much to do."

The two leaders shook hands with the General Manager and strolled up the street with an air of importance they could not help. Until they had turned into the Company's housing estate, away from the main street and its eyes, they did not discuss at all the unprecedented occurrence.

"You were very formal, Rafael," Gil said.

"Look! No one would expect us to refuse to allow him to sit down. But to continue in friendship and to accept his drinks, no!"

"All the same, there is much to discuss if he is willing."

"At a café table? That would be beneath his dignity."

"He is a man who carries his dignity about with him."

Rafael Garay silently agreed and resented it. Respect for the enemy was an unnecessary complication of his boycott, so deadly simple if it were kept simple. He stopped in his compact stride and flung out the palm of his hand.

"If he wishes to fight, I hold him there!"

The gesture was for himself — an affirmation of faith. He saw that it was so undeniably true that he could safely feel pity for his victim if nothing more.

"Suppose he does not wish to fight and offers guarantees for the future?"

"What future? We will not forget the dead."

"Who says I forget them?"

"I take it back, brother. A little frankness between friends — that is all."

Gil pressed his arm.

"Believe me, Rafael, after you and Chepe no one loved Catalina more than I. But Cabo Desierto — one must remember that there is a world outside it."

Rafael went on alone to his house, one of a casual un-regimented cluster which stood close under the hillside beneath the first hairpin of the road. His son was in the yard, heartily flooding the cans, tubs and troughs of flowers which Catalina had watered daily. Few of them seemed likely to recover from neglect.

"Have you had a good day?" he asked.

It was Catalina's invariable question when Rafael returned. To hear it again from Chepe reminded him how keenly he would have missed the repetition had she for once omitted it.

"So-so."

"The committee, papacito?"

From one so small the word sounded overlarge; but that was natural enough. The committee was a great, vague unknown which swallowed up his father.

"No, not the committee. I have been talking to the General Manager."

Rafael, as any other man, was bound to show his pride when speaking to wife or son. In public he would have affected an air of unconcern.

"He is kind. I told you so."

"Well, now I believe all you said."

"Didn't you then?"

"When one is young, one does not always know the difference between play and truth."

"I do. I tell the truth."

"Yes? As when you speared the whale and it died?"

"It was a whale and I stabbed it hard and my stick went in," the boy answered boldly.

No getting out of that! And indeed it was a whale, a very small whale, and Chepe had been the first to find it stranded on the foreshore. Whether it died before he poked it with his stick was, Catalina had said, beside the point.

"And so you really spoke to Don Mateo on the night he arrived? What did he say?"

"He said I must not go home past the police at the gate."

"And then?"

"He stayed a little longer. He played with the fish, too, and went to bed."

"But why did you go there?"

The boy hesitated.

"I thought he might kill people like the other."

"You walked all the way up to his house?"

"I only meant to go up the hill. You said you would be late. So I jumped a truck on the bend. I go up and down as I like. But the truck went all the way to the old field. When it stopped, the driver got out. I did not know him, so I got out too and followed him."

"Chepe, that is not right. I have told you that you are not to watch grown-up people secretly."

"Not with girls, you said. I saw him lift up some boards and then he went back to the truck and started to unload boxes and carry them away."

"What was in the boxes?" Rafael asked, knowing his son.

"Like in the box you told me not to touch. So while he was away at the boards I took one and climbed into Don Mateo's garden."

"A cartridge?"

"No. The sort you light and throw at policemen."

Rafael was startled by so plain a statement. When and from what conversation had the boy picked that up? He was as full of curiosity as a mouse in a tool shed, unsuspected until one caught a glimpse of sensitive whiskers and one bright eye. His father fell back on the feeble excuse that killing policemen was wrong and one didn't light it.

"That was what Don Mateo said," Chepe answered, as if his opinion of the General Manager had now been confirmed by superior authority.

Rafael's passionate respect for his son stopped him from exclaiming what he thought of this revelation. Though a drop of cold sweat was trickling down his ribs, he solemnly agreed that Don Mateo was right. Chepe, relieved to find that attempted murder was taken so calmly by all concerned, came out triumphantly with the whole story.

For Rafael the problem was how to show his gratitude. Whatever his feelings, a person of honor must have decent manners. But to call upon this Don Mateo at his office or his house was impossible, and to write an appropriate letter needed the assistance of someone more experienced who could never be trusted to keep it quiet. In any case he had to admit that his son had seen explosives and listened to some boasting of their value in defense against the police. More awkward still were those two rifle shots at Birenfield, which he had aimed only to frighten but with a hand so shaking with anger that the first had smashed the arm of his chair.

To hell with it! Manners would just have to stay on his conscience. Meanwhile, who was the driver of the truck and what was he doing with dynamite? The committee had only a few kilos collected from weekend fishermen who had nicked them from railway stores in the Capital for use in the more sheltered coves to the north. None of the sticks had been distributed.

"Where did he hide the boxes, Chepe? Can you show me?"

"It was very dark, papacito, and I could not see the number of the well. He took the third road and had his lights out."

"Where did he stop?"

"Not far from 58."

The world outside Cabo Desierto, which Gil Delgado tended to mention more often than at first, was opening up too far. Rafael's vision of it was a hostile mass compressing the workers into ever greater solidarity. But the eccentricities of this perceptive General Manager did not fit in; nor did the behavior of the stranger. That he really was a stranger was fairly certain. Chepe knew the whole field by sight, if not by name.

"Are you tired?"

"No, papacito. I have been sitting still all day."

"For ten minutes, perhaps! Then let us eat a bite and go!"

The boy and his father climbed the slope to the sharp curve of the road where Chepe was accustomed to jump a truck and then up the steep footpath, well worn by men taking a shortcut home, which led from one bend to another, across the dip between the ridges and on up to the abandoned field. In old days there would have been plenty of movement on road and path, but now there was only the tall outline of Rafael carrying Chepe on his shoulders.

On the second ridge the derricks, being darker than the night, were clear enough, but their order had been complicated by the dismantling of useful machinery and a mess of beams, old iron and drill pipe left behind on the ground. Where the truck had stopped beyond the old bailing well numbered 58 was plain, and Chepe was sure of the direction in which the driver had walked; but once engaged in the derelict forest where earth, concrete and every object was equally black with oil, he was no longer sure of anything except that the boxes had been hidden under some boards. When pressed with questions he merely got muddled between the ranks of the fifties and the ranks of the thirties.

It seemed unlikely that the driver would have taken the road he did if he was bound for the thirties. However, they were not far away and worth a visit in the hope that Chepe would recognize some landmark. The offshore breeze was busy among the rigs, creaking loose struts and banging notice boards with enough noise to cover the padding of canvas-and-rubber shoes as Rafael and Chepe moved carefully over the litter. Beyond the next well, numbered 32A, somebody else was not so careful. There was a thud and a whispered blast of curses. Father and son dropped behind a pump and watched a cone of light gliding over and traversing the broken ground. The man behind the torch passed close to the pump and Rafael recognized him, more by his bearing than his face. It was undoubtedly Lorenzo, the General Manager's driver.

When the intruder had returned to the road, Rafael asked:

"Was it Lorenzo you saw that night?"

"No. I am sure."

"A Company truck or a town truck, Chepe?"

"Company."

"And the number?"

"I did not look."

Lorenzo was not hiding another consignment of explosives or withdrawing any from stock. His movements made it obvious that he was searching for the right place just as they were, and it seemed probable that this was one of several repeated attempts undertaken when his day's work was over and he knew that he would not be needed. Such obstinacy fitted his character. It was his duty to find the stuff and he couldn't. But duty to whom? Lorenzo was a loyal servant with no sympathy for the boycott. He might well have been ordered to look for the source of Chepe's stick. But how did Don Mateo know it was in the old field? And if he did know, one would have thought that the search would be made in daylight by a party from the office under Mr. Thorpe, not secretly at night.

"Chepe, did you tell the Manager where you got it?"

"No, papacito. He did not ask me."

It was a waste of time to stay longer and keep Chepe out of bed. The boards were undiscoverable. Anyway the carpenter's shop had never been asked to make any sort of lid for a hole. Rafael put the whole uncomfortable business out of mind, happy for the moment in the companionship of his son. They slid home hand in hand down the steep footpath, laughing like boys returning from some forbidden adventure. Only when Chepe was asleep and no other breathing sounded did Rafael's mood change to self-reproach — not blaming himself for what he had achieved, which was right a thousand times, but for accepting leadership when he was nothing but a good carpenter. To kill the field had been easy, yes, and triumphant, but not turning out as simple a death as that of a man who stayed dead. It was more like the burning of a hillside. On the surface everything died and underground everything was alive — silent and complicated as the unintelligible power of the Three Sentinels.

FIVE. For the pioneers of Cabo Desierto, oil had been easier to tap than water. The nearest of the short rivers of the coast was thirty miles away and useless — violent after mountain storms, reduced to paddle pools or nothing for the rest of the year. Faith, finance and an army of labor, easier to recruit than to feed, drained the high, misty bogs, tunneled and dammed and were rewarded beyond expectation. In Mat Darlow's youth the overflow from

76

the tanks on the old field and the town reservoir formed a respectable stream running into the Pacific.

This precious waste was impounded in the Charca and put to work. Step by step the coast was irrigated to establish the Company Farm. When all drilling stopped in the old field and again there was water to spare, the Company formed a Cooperative of individuals and groups willing to transform the desert as a profitable leisure activity. Both the Company Farm and the communal lands turned out to be first-class investments, supplying the field with more than half its food well under the blackmailing prices of the wholesale merchants in the Capital.

If ever there were an example of enlightened capitalism digging its own grave by a generous gesture, this, Mat thought, was it! One of his first visits had been to the central market to see for himself how the community carried on without money. Well, strictly speaking, it didn't. Imports had dried up and shopkeepers were in a bad way, but relief funds and a small dole distributed by the Cooperative dribbled just enough cash into circulation for a workable economy. The boycott could last indefinitely provided the men were really determined to live as peasants.

After the market he had inspected production — if one could call it inspection when it was only staring. The landscape of green fields and blue sea, set against gray desert and tawny mountain, was artificial as a painting on the neutral walls of a gallery with a similar brilliant life of its own. In the Cooperative's section of this startling oasis maize, lucerne and vegetables showed the effect of intensive, personal care. There was even wheat, though far too heavy in the ear and blotched by the channels of the wind. He had never really believed that Cabo Desierto could live without oil, but this was not at all the woolly project of an agricultural commune which, in London, seemed sure to collapse. The overwhelming, verdant fact formed a base so strong that it invited violence in attack and defense.

Between the fields and the sea small gangs were steadily at work in the evening sun extending the irrigation channels. He longed to stop and talk to them, but questions at that early stage could only arouse suspicion; so he had driven on to the Company Farm and spent an hour with the manager, Manuel Uriarte, a young Chilean happily aware that he was one of the few human beings to see dreams come true. After looking over the dairy herd, the arable, the citrus orchards just coming into bearing, he congratulated the creator of it all on his marvelous experiment. Experiments were few, Uriarte answered. This was simply what happened with scientific management and enough water. He was prepared to grow three crops a year of anything which would stand twelve hours of tropical sun at sea level.

"That's possible for the communal lands, too?"

"Of course."

"And before the boycott the men took a serious interest?"

"Serious as children in a laboratory. They have offered to pay my salary if the Company won't."

"What will they use for money?"

"Not an idea! But I'm staying even if they pay me in beef and bananas."

Mat assured him that no such Utopia was likely. The

Three Sentinels would never be allowed to stand still in a bucolic dream.

"I'm told the water will not be cut off."

It was a question rather than a comment. Uriarte's steady voice would, Mat guessed, be well known to doctors. Am I going to die? Will everything go irretrievably back to desert in three weeks?

At this time of year it was possible, for the high dam in the Cordillera was delivering only enough for the town. In the past week the overflow from the Charca had stopped, and its level would now fall fast for a couple of months without a hope of restoring it. Thus it was easy to break the boycott by opening the pipes in the dam abutments — or would be easy if there were a company of troops, ruthless and well armed, to prevent desperate men, faced by surrender or starvation, from closing the valves.

The Government would never dare to use such force and the field was not to be taken in by bluff. Mat's early reports to London had emphasized the calm confidence of the boycott committee. Henry Constantinides accepted his reading of the situation and in a private letter asked for recommendations for his own eyes only. Mat was aware that his reply rambled too widely over characters and atmosphere, but his summing-up was, he hoped, precise.

"The short cut to peace is to pull the carpet out from under them," he wrote. "We should work out a scheme whereby the houses are conveyed on long lease to the Municipality or a Housing Corporation. A man could then be sacked for reasons of discipline or redundancy but could not be turned out of Cabo Desierto so long as he continued to pay his rent.

79

"The field is just as arrogant and independent as ever it was, so I cannot guarantee that such a move would break the boycott at once, but it might split the committee. If a minority still refuses to forgive the loss of the women and insists — as a point of honor or obstinacy — in growing potatoes, I am ready to allow them to do so with my blessing.

"The Company must always remember that Cabo Desierto is no longer a wasteland for adventurers; it is home."

That was the point. Considering whether he had put it forcibly enough, Mat stood at his office window from which he could see nothing but tops of palms which prevented the vulgarity of human beings from intruding. At least he supposed that was the intention. It seemed unlikely that the office was designed to prevent the General Manager idly watching movement on the avenue. He would have preferred the headquarters building to be down at the port where it used to be. Bloody popular he would find himself if he suggested it! Such a move was the equivalent of closing the London Wall office and sending Henry out to Bermondsey, bowler hat and all. Anyway, how the various offices were distributed was, at the moment, about as important as the contract — if there was one — for arranging the flowers in the entrance hall.

An idea! The boycott committee could ship flowers to the Capital and get some much needed cash. He was continually fascinated by the engaging lunacy of living off the communal lands. He had far more projects for them — which he certainly was not going to tell to Messrs. Garay and Delgado — than for setting the oil flowing.

"Who does the flowers, Pilar?" he asked.

"The gardeners. Several of them, I think."

Evidently she took them for granted like the supply of stationery. Yet it tickled his perverse sense of romance to imagine those gardeners with earth between their toes padding into the building when only cleaners were about and arranging — quite as delicately as any females rushing around London and pretending that ordinary good taste was an abstruse art — the harvest of their coarse, copper hands.

"That is what the slippers are for?"

"What slippers?"

"Under the ledge by the entrance."

"You're always asking questions I can't answer, Mr. Darlow."

He suspected that she was exasperated by his collection of inessential details upon which imagination could go to work. Neatly arranged facts and a decision were what she seemed to like.

"You answer a hundred questions a week, Pilar."

"About policy, yes, and routine and the staff."

"Well, that covers it."

"Not your private curiosities."

"April showers. Come on me suddenly."

"About such little things and never about things you ought to want to know."

"For example?"

She thought for a moment, trying to pin her accusation to a fact.

"Yes, here's one! Why do you never ask me about Mr. Birenfield?"

"At my age, Pilar, I could take a Birenfield to pieces and put all the bits back where they belonged."

This time he had really annoyed her, and he could see that she was not going to let him get away with it. How old would she be? Twenty-five, twenty-seven years younger than he? He watched her mouth. She had half a mind to argue, and the other half ready to walk out.

"Then what was he doing on the old field all alone at night?"

"Meeting somebody secretly whom he didn't want to take home."

"Really, Mr. Darlow! You know there was a blank wall between him and the men."

"Then somebody from the Capital."

"He flew there nearly every week, so he didn't need secret meetings here. Or do you think he had a girl?"

"Not on the old field," he laughed. "How do you know this?"

"I don't. I only add up nothings like any other woman. You depend on your eyes, Mr. Darlow. We use our ears."

"Oil-wives' gossip?"

"If you like. But it's not what they say; it's what they don't say and look as if they could. That's a kind of slippers-under-the-ledge, too."

"Gave nothing away himself?"

"Never, if he could help it. Didn't you find that among your bits and pieces?"

"Gateson probably knows what he was doing up there. I'll ask him."

"Shouldn't you know the answer yourself first?"

"Oh, Gateson is all right. A bit jealous of course, but that's natural."

"Very natural."

She held his eyes and, by God, she meant to! A splendid woman she was, with a high-breasted body like that of a Greek Aphrodite, and the same rounded, columnar middle instead of a hymenopterous waist. That suspicion of hair on the upper lip had always attracted him. Well, no time and place for those complications now! One must live on one's memories.

And, anyway, he did not trust her. The ears she mentioned missed little. Birenfield was right to be secretive. She had too many right-wing relatives in high places who would welcome any leakage of the new manager's intentions. To set the oil flowing again was a mere half of his task; the ultimate value of Cabo Desierto had also to be considered, and that was bound to be affected not only by what he did but how he did it.

He was even reluctant to give his handwritten letter to Pilar, leaving her to make up the mail for the Company's plane to the Capital; the security of an envelope was not enough. So he relinquished the unprofitable office window and hastily scribbled a few more private letters to account for his time — he had some trouble in thinking of suitable recipients — and handed them over. Then with Henry's letter in his pocket he drove down to the port knowing that a launch was due to sail in the afternoon under the skipper who had carried him to Cabo Desierto.

He was sure of his judgment in dealing with a plain seaman, perfectly content to tell him to airmail his letter in the Capital next morning; he knew it would be done though he had spent only a few hours with the man. He accused himself of blind prejudice against Pilar Alvarez merely because she was well groomed and an aristocratic showpiece. How many times had he been told that he did not understand women? Well, the wise course was to accept it as a fact and take no risks.

Gonzalez, now. He must not be ignored. Politeness oiled his dirty wheels without washing them. He would be hurt if he learned that the General Manager had been hanging around the port with no obviously urgent business and had not called on him.

He could not respect the police captain; the man was a coward and had little control over his men. Their comings and goings in the town were by tacit permission of the boycott committee — with exception of those catastrophic and secret excursions to the shacks beyond the refinery. No, Gonzalez was not fit to command a rabbit hutch. He should, Mat thought, have been a plainclothes security agent working on his own. Perhaps he had been, and too successful. It was conceivable that his weary eyes had seen more than was good for his health and that he had quickly taken refuge in the uniformed branch.

Captain Gonzalez dismissed a visitor with affectionate pats on the shoulder, shut the door, sent for coffee, and produced a really excellent Havana. Faultless! He could do a lot more execution with his excellent manners than the damned great gun in his lopsided belt.

Mat received the usual lecture on the unnecessary risks that he was taking, and replied that there weren't any, that the boycott committee considered him a simple, friendly fellow wasting his time.

"Far from simple, Don Mateo. And when they discover it there must be some temptation to have you out of the way."

"An unfortunate accident?"

"That would be difficult to arrange convincingly."

"Why?"

"Because your movements are unpredictable. Frankly I never know where you are going to be till you have left. If only you were not so impulsive! You are the despair of my agents."

Typical Gonzalez! A most intelligent comment followed by a pretense of efficiency. He hadn't got any agents. At Cabo Desierto everyone knew everyone else. Any local inhabitant found chatting too confidentially with police posts or calling on Gonzalez without good reason would be rolled through the door of the customs shed in a dirty oil drum. Mat was prepared to bet that all the captain ever did was to get himself telephoned by Pilar or Pepe or the doorman at headquarters.

"You have taken to driving your car yourself. Do so sometimes but not always!"

"You distrust Lorenzo?"

"Not at all, Don Mateo! He is faithful to his uniform. I merely say that it should never be certain whether you will be alone in the car or not."

"It's true that I should be more careful not to hurt Lorenzo's pride. Any other suggestions?"

Gonzalez hesitated, fiddling with his papers as if somewhere among them might be a suggestion which had nothing to do with him.

"It is always easier to arrange accidents than to prevent them," he said.

"I thought you liked Rafael Garay."

"We are beyond likes and dislikes. If a rock cannot be moved it must be smashed."

Like a rock. Where had he heard that before? Said it to Thorpe, of course! Not a very good illustration. Garay really was one. He himself felt more like a mud pool, reliably covering God knows what. He reminded Gonzalez that there would only be small souvenirs left of the police if Garay suffered an accident.

"But let us suppose I could prove who was the criminal."

"Not me, I hope. The Company's funeral fund doesn't run to General Managers."

"Neither of us, Don Mateo. The Union. I have been told that if I take no notice of any agent of theirs they are prepared to pay."

It was essential to preserve a mildly benevolent expression. Apparently he had the confidence of the dirty little rat, and that was to be valued even at the cost of being considered a possible fellow gangster.

"Garay is hated as much as that?"

"One cannot throw Union delegates into the harbor without making enemies."

"Why not Delgado, too?"

"They are not afraid of him. Delgado is ambitious. But Garay — one can only compare him to a mad priest with the faithful at his feet."

"What have you replied?"

"Nothing. I don't know yet what they intend. Put yourself in my place! Where am I? Who am I? There is no one but you I trust."

"Your chiefs?"

"A blind eye, Don Mateo! No doubt this was mentioned to them. No doubt they made the proper motions of disgust. And in parting they whispered that it would be best to try that little rat Gonzalez."

The bitter coincidence that Gonzalez, dropping all pride, should have quoted the very word which Mat in his own mind had found for him instantly aroused his pity for the man. What a choice for the job — but possibly wise! The captain could be trusted to do as little as possible and keep up a façade of decency. A stronger man might play hell with the whole situation.

"I will take your orders," Gonzalez went on. "You have only to say what you want."

"What I want, friend, is Garay's word or his signature, and a dead man cannot give it."

"Look, Don Mateo! Up on your hill and down here none of the rest of us count. Me, I am only a policeman in the first act of a play, there to make them all laugh a little and be afraid a little. But in the third act you and Garay will be very much alone."

"Tragedy or comedy?"

"Tragedy if you do not get rid of him."

Well, that was cheerful! An interesting fellow, Gonzalez. How could a man be so sensitive without any conscience whatever? His unexpectedly intimate conversation had certainly opened up some new vistas.

Mat had left the Union out of all calculations as completely powerless, overlooking the fact that the pompous did not like being powerless. Certainly Dave Gunner didn't. What was all that about organized labor being the only hope of stability? While in the Capital he had dutifully called on the Secretary of the Union who rambled on about the excellent cooperation between Birenfield and himself, hoping that it would continue. Exactly what cooperation there could be when the field had expelled the Union and been excommunicated in return it was hard to see, but the man now appeared to have had something definite in mind — possibly, as Gonzalez had hinted, strong-arm tactics directed against the uncontrollable leaders of the boycott. His hatred of them had been obvious.

At home he was greeted by Pepe with the news that Mr. Thorpe had telephoned to ask if he and his wife could come round for a drink. What a day for cloaked motives on the back stairs! It would have been more natural to invite the General Manager to call if he were free. He saw why they didn't. His car standing outside the Thorpes' bungalow would invite comment up and down the executive ghetto, especially if no one else had been invited to meet him. Damn these women! But it was fair enough — even admirable — that they should all be jockeying for their husbands in an emergency with an unforeseeable end.

He was reminded of Mrs Gateson and her inexplicable question about Lorenzo. There was a very faint wisp of a smell. The police captain's remark that he was faithful to his uniform was on the face of it decisive. He meant neither more nor less, but it seemed to need expanding a bit. Mat held Pepe in conversation, hoping for something more revealing than Lorenzo's file which merely confirmed that he was reliable and that Birenfield had picked him from the mechanics' pool to be his personal driver.

Didn't Pepe and Amelia ever miss the Capital? No, Pepe said, Cabo Desierto was home and if the local cinema would only show films that did not disgust a man of experience he would have no complaint.

"And the Company? You are content?"

"Very content. It has treated me well. Amelia and I — we have security and our economies for when we are old."

How often was loyalty nothing more than the removal of all fear for the future? And anyway why shouldn't it be? Mutual trust was a fine thing whatever the reason for it.

"Lorenzo, too?"

"For him Mr. Birenfield was God."

There was a shade of contempt in the answer. Pepe had already dropped hints of his feeling for Birenfield, so Mat put the direct question.

"You did not like him?"

"Neither I nor Amelia. A good man, very polite, very easy to work for. But never an enthusiasm! Life — he had no grumbles and no praise. I will tell you an absurdity. The first morning you were here you had your papaya and after I saw your face I said to Amelia: 'This one is no Birenfield. We shall enjoy giving him pleasure.' "

"You do give it, Pepe, and a thousand thanks! But, to be fair, the world cannot go on without its Birenfields. I suppose that is why they bother to stay in it. What did this one have which attracted Lorenzo?"

"Nothing, man! Lorenzo must attach himself, and I have told you that Mr. Birenfield was very polite. An order, and Lorenzo was happy!"

"And Mrs. Birenfield?"

"Like him. And since she could find little to do in Cabo Desierto she would spend half the day in bed, talking to Amelia or Mrs. Gateson."

Not much alternative perhaps. At least Birenfield had something to come home to. Wonder if he talked over the problems of the Three Sentinels or gave them up and joined her in bed! At any rate he wasn't limited to the brilliant emptiness of the night.

When the Thorpes arrived, they seemed unsure that they were justified in inviting themselves. Mat made them very welcome, envying their partnership. Part of Thorpe's reputation for knowing names and faces was undoubtedly due to his wife.

"It was Jane who wanted to see you," he explained. "But I thought I'd walk over with her."

She would have been well liked in the Cabo Desierto of thirty years earlier, Mat thought — a fair, motherly woman, squarish rather than full, who could have run the canteens for them and had every American pulling out family snaps from his wallet within five minutes.

"I've got a message for you," she said. "But I don't want you to think I'm on the wrong side."

"I don't know which is the wrong one, Mrs. Thorpe. There ain't no Salvation Army to tell us."

She smiled and thanked heaven she had not got to deal with London and the Government, but just Cabo Desierto.

"I got on so well with poor Catalina. And I was in at the end, you see. So whenever I meet Rafael Garay he goes out of his way to talk to me. He wants a private interview with you, but he won't come to your house or office."

"I've told her I don't like it," Thorpe interrupted. "It's all over the town that Garay and Delgado paid you a drink, so if they want to talk they can do it again."

"No, not of their own accord. I took them by surprise. Where does he suggest we meet, Mrs. Thorpe?"

"He said he was working on the communal pigpens every evening if you happened to be passing."

"Our pigs or theirs?"

"Theirs. They bought them from the Company long before the boycott."

He got her talking about Garay. She wondered whether Catalina had grabbed him as just right for her taste or whether she had formed his character. He was too honest, she thought, to be an agitator; the job had been forced on him by general acclaim. Ray Thorpe added that Garay would make a first-class soldier — a formidable guerrilla leader if it ever came to street fighting again — but he wasn't any sort of politician.

"No. Too much human affection," Mat said. "That's why he daren't give an inch."

"Affection! Affection for what?"

"I only heard it in his voice. For his fellows, I suppose, and of course his son."

"Now, how on earth do you know about Chepe?" Jane asked.

"I've run across him."

"That child needs a firm hand. He's a law to himself."

"Better than other people's."

"Not at seven years old," she protested.

"Do you see him? Often?"

"You sound jealous, Mr. Darlow. No, he just turns up

sometimes and looks at me with big eyes and goes away."

"Poor little blighter!"

"Rafael gives him all the love that Catalina did. Chepe is his treasure. But he hasn't enough time now."

"Does he feel his life is in any danger?"

"He hasn't mentioned it. From whom?"

"Well, me — for one of several."

"Of course not! I don't see how you have worked it, but he trusts you."

"It's mutual. I shall have the police guards removed altogether from headquarters and my house."

"You mustn't do that!" she exclaimed. "You'll just create resentment."

"Why? It's a gesture I can afford to make. The police are no earthly use."

"But the mothers like to see them. And if you take the guards off your house, Bill Gateson and the others will have to."

"They can do as they wish."

"No, they can't, Mr. Darlow. They'll look such cowards if they don't do the same as you."

She might be right, but reducing the temperature was what mattered, not popularity at the country club.

"Blind ahead with whatever you decide, but keep your eyes open!" Thorpe said. "You and Garay are beginning to remind me of a couple of snipers I once saw — so bloody fascinated by each other that neither looked to his flank."

Mat let that go. Ray Thorpe saw everything in terms of attack, but there was truth in what he said. At present it was only possible to blind ahead, probing as he went. As for his flanks, they were all uncovered.

However, the invitation to the pigpens could not be refused. Dignity was nonsense, and the Superintendent's suspicion of a trap did not fit his wife's reading of Garay. So the following evening he drove out along the lush communal lands smelling as if they received the rainfall of green jungle. Damn it, this was a high-pressure oil field, not a millionaire's *estancia!* There was one sure way to smash the boycott: by emptying the Charca. He wondered if the men in the distance, sweating with pick and shovel and bags of cement to extend the channels, realized it as clearly as he.

He left his car and walked over to the communal pigs. It was on the sun shelters that Rafael Garay was working. The model pens and sties did not look as if repairs would be needed for years. In the darkness under the leaf thatch the face and arms of the carpenter were invisible. A white cotton shirt was knocking in staples without any occupant.

Mat leaned on a rail until the white eyes rolled in his direction.

"What's new?" he asked.

Rafael came over to him. Under the dark face the stocky, powerful figure was that of a Spanish peasant.

"Nothing to please you, Mr. Manager. I only wished to thank you with all my heart."

"But that does please me. What for?"

"My son has told me all the truth of what happened on the night of your arrival. There is no one in the world who would have done what you did."

"Nothing special, man! It's just that I have no children of my own. Don't punish him! What courage!"

93

"I want you to know that he did not get his dynamite from me."

"Then I hope you know where he did get it."

Rafael hesitated. "You need not have a care," he said. "I give you a whole sea of gratitude, and go with God!"

"When may I meet your committee?"

"Whenever you wish. You have only to let me know."

"Meanwhile, consider this with your mates! The boycott does not hurt us as much as you believe. The value of the oil we are losing is nothing compared to the value of the field."

"It has no value. You cannot sell a Company which will never have oil."

"Never is a big word, friend. If you won't work, the Government may send a cruiser — and a shipload of men who will."

"Then they will have to deport the lot of us by force."

A blank wall. There was no longer any government this side of the Iron Curtain which would dare to mow down its workers — let alone a bunch of so-called liberals hanging on to power and continually threatened by an explosion from the left. A bloody wonder the politicians didn't order prayers in the churches for Cabo Desierto's General Manager!

And here was another decision to be taken which could irrevocably alter the future. Ray Thorpe's remark, lumping himself and Garay together, had some bearing on it. If there were a sniper out to the flank, this black spellbinder had much the better chance of spotting him.

"By the way, Don Rafael," he said, using the prefix of courteous equality, "it was not dynamite; it was gelignite."

"What is that?"

"Much the same, but for cutting steel."

"From the Company store?"

"No. We haven't any."

SIX. The last red segment of the sun vanished into the Pacific as Mat Darlow started down to the sports pavilion for a first meeting with the boycott committee; yet lights behind east-facing windows were already on by the time his car reached the sea front. It was no wonder, he thought, that so harsh and exact a world, where the only twilight was the mountain shadow which delayed dawn, forced upon those who lived in it a violent simplicity.

96

For the last forty-eight hours he had been mulling over Henry's reply to his private letter. Silky as always. But at least the Managing Director was backing him — with presumably the approval of some nebula of money evolving through the telephones of the City until ready to condense into golden reality.

"I agree with you over the housing," Henry had written. "We will accept in principle any scheme you recommend so long as it can be presented to the shareholders as the enlightened policy of a forward-looking company. Details of course will be for the lawyers.

"You have made an excellent start. I know that partly through the diplomats, partly through Dave Gunner who thinks you are missing opportunities. Thank God for north country bluntness! Dave can always be trusted not to notice when he has let a cat out of a bag. He has his own lines out. Government or one of his International Labor connections?

"You should keep in mind three facts about Gunner:

"1. He has spent a lifetime in the belief that every society must be run in the interests of the industrial workers and that Unions can do no wrong. Mass revolt is anathema — especially when elected leaders are made to swim.

"2. He hates land. Food should be organized and provided by governments. In that he agrees with Stalin, but God forbid that I should ever point it out!

"3. He is alarmed by any proposal to give away assets to what he calls dagoes. I, being an immoral capitalist, take a longer view. A contented community adds enormously to the value of Cabo Desierto and until we have it I will not

97

advise acceptance of any offer for the field. If that means allowing a chap to get out of oil into potatoes, I am perfectly prepared to help and encourage.

"Don't bother about Dave! He has the tendency of a weak man to square his chin, but at this end we can vote him down. I am more worried by what might happen at your end and can't put a name to my suspicions."

A cautious letter like the label on a box of pills. May be prescribed with confidence but watch out for contraindications! Still, there was warmth and support. It occurred to Mat — not for the first time in his life — that he met with approval at the top and the bottom and mistrust in the middle.

Lorenzo stopped the car at the gate to the sports ground and impassively opened the door for the General Manager. Though there was nothing obsequious about his bearing or legs, from the waist up he always seemed to be waiting for orders. The loose gathering of oil workers returned Mat's greetings as he walked through them, showing neither enmity nor encouragement; he might have been a groundsman come to mark out the football field. That was more or less what he wanted. He had announced his intention as merely asking and answering questions on such minor points as canteens, imports, use of launches and the school, and had firmly turned down a suggestion that the Mayor should ceremoniously take the chair. The meeting would then have developed into a competition of eloquence, hardening attitudes and settling nothing.

Fourteen of the leaders were there to receive him. The table round which they sat was intelligently arranged with Rafael Garay at one end and himself, flanked by Gil

Delgado, at the other. Though some members of the committee were cold and smug and some inclined to be over-hearty from embarrassment, he was surprised at the deference shown to him.

For an hour relations were easy enough. With pad and pencil in front of him, he might have been, say, a borough engineer at a meeting of tenants, ready to agree to some of their requirements and to explain why others could not be met. Garay was his natural self. He gave the impression of a man so sure of his policy that he could afford to be reasonable, even grateful. Delgado, on the other hand, several times struck a note of hostility. Why? A possible reading was that he had to pretend more solidarity than he really felt.

"Wine is agreed then," Delgado said, "on condition that you do not expect us to hold out our mugs outside the church door. But what about water? Will you sign a contract for our supply?"

Nobody else spoke. For a moment Mat could hear the monotony of the surf. Evidently this was unexpected.

"A lot of good that would be to you! If you put an end to the Company, what value has the Company's signature?"

That rammed home one of the illogicalities of their stubbornness. If there was to be no more oil, who or what would own Cabo Desierto? Delgado left it at that, his only comment being a half-smile of contempt directed down the table. It looked as if he accepted the answer and was ready to let it stay in the minds of the committee. The contempt could be for them.

"Listen, Mr. Manager!" Garay exclaimed. "No one will ever drive us from our homes."

"No need to repeat it. I agree. No one will. But you must excuse me, Don Rafael. I did not mean to break our understanding that the boycott would not be discussed. Now, before I leave, may I ask one question? Tell me to go to the devil if you like! What exactly are your present relations with your Union?"

The committee erupted. At least six indignant voices bellowed simultaneously, with the howl of a passing jet from high note to low, that they had no relations with the dirty sons of whores.

"You pay your dues?"

"Never again!" Garay answered.

"And if a senior delegate were to come and help us with negotiations?"

"Into the harbor! And this time no launch to fish him out!"

"That's hard on me. I am forced to be the Company, your Union, the State and myself all at the same time."

"Then you won't need any stamps on the letters, Mr. Manager," Delgado said and raised a general laugh.

"Very true. But mine are delivered and yours are not."

The retort went home with no reply but muttering. It was time to remind them that he had power as well as goodwill. He thanked the committee and got up. Except for his calculated slip, terms of peace had never been mentioned at all. He wondered how many of them were secretly disappointed.

As he strolled away from the pavilion to his car, speed and intentness of thinking carried on. He had no longer to concentrate on the dark, set faces, the watchful eyes waiting for any threat, and so his searching mind switched into the allied problems which he alone could solve. Henry's vague suspicions. The approaches made to Gonzalez. All dropped into place without anything he could really call reasoning.

One couldn't put it past a jealous Union to plan the assassination of Garay, but it was damned unlikely. As for Dave Gunner, murder would never be included or even imagined, whatever squaring of his chin he had in mind. Gonzalez was telling the truth all right about turning a blind eye to any Union agent, but he had either guessed at the real objective or been deliberately put off the scent.

He turned back from the car as if he had left some personal possession behind and called to Garay who with two or three others was politely waiting by the porch of the pavilion to see him drive off. An instinctive impulse, yes! But the fault, if it was one, had not led him far wrong up to the present.

"A quick word!" he said as they met on the path half-way. "Any luck?"

"With what? You think you will have luck because you show your face?"

"With Chepe's toffee, I meant. It seemed to me you didn't know where he got it."

"It could be for you, Mr. Manager."

It could indeed. The reply was unexpectedly brutal, but probably the only cause was resentment of himself and his question. The man was naturally on edge after a meeting in which he had been given little chance to show his hatred of the Company.

"Or for you."

"No one would dare. I do not count. But no one would dare. So much for your threats!"

"No threat from me, friend. I need you."

"You? Why?"

"For one thing, nobody else can make a decent coffin."

"The things you say! We are not bandits. I have told you that you needn't have a care."

"Then think a little! If these explosives are not for you or me, could they be for the Charca?"

"Who would do that except the Company?"

"That's for you to tell me. The Union, perhaps? Any of you can see me whenever you wish."

Rafael returned to the pavilion and reported that Don Mateo had suggested as an afterthought that no one need feel embarrassment in calling at the office. As soon as he was alone with Gil Delgado he repeated the obscure hint but could not bring himself to disclose Chepe's story of hidden explosives. His son's affairs were intensely private and to be investigated only by himself.

"It is a trick," Delgado replied at once. "He means to cut off our water and pin the blame on someone else."

That might be so. Rafael accepted that his colleague was cleverer than he. On the other hand Gil had not the gift of trust. One could not begin to explain to him that a man was not to be judged wholly by his words or even by his eyes. He was there and you were there and a thing passed from one to the other.

"There are no Union agents among us," Gil went on. "But remember that not all of us like poking with a hoe and Don Mateo must know it."

"I do not understand him," Rafael said. "He seems half on our side."

He expected to be laughed at, but Gil replied impatiently:

"Of course he is! He still hopes that we will return to work without damage or bloodshed."

Well, they would not, and let him hope! Rafael was irritated by all the subtle contradictions of this man who sat back and almost encouraged the development of a Cabo Desierto without oil.

Gil was right on one point. The Union had no active agents among the workers. There might be sympathizers, but not one of them would agree to blowing up the Charca or had the knowledge to do it. The man who, unknown to himself, had given Chepe a ride in his truck came from outside. If he had any collaborator in Cabo Desierto it must be Lorenzo or some other trusted servant of the management.

Rafael slipped away to the empty beach beyond the tank farm where he strolled up and down among the refuse, stopping from time to time to allow for the instinctive gesture of scratching his head. That the stranger had come overland was most improbable. He had brought a small truckload of boxes as well as himself. Then he must have come in one of the company launches with the connivance of Gonzalez. During the boycott all passengers had to show their identity cards and explain their business to the police on the quay. God alone knew what Gonzalez did, all dressed up in his office, but one could always hear two typewriters clacking.

The arrangements had obviously been made before the

new General Manager's arrival, but whatever Gonzalez knew, Don Mateo would. So Gil might be partly right. Yet Don Mateo was to be trusted. That was the only certain fact: a man. Then if the Company and its launches were not involved, the explosives could only have arrived by fishing boat.

Next day Rafael began inquiries. The operation got on his nerves. He had no faith in his ability to ask questions and conceal his motive, for no sort of intrigue had ever disturbed the plain honesty of a life spent between Catalina and the carpenter's bench. The fish buyers in the market talked freely, finding it natural that he should show curiosity about supplies. Not so many boats put in, they said, as before the boycott, and only when they had a lot of coarse fish which Cabo Desierto could afford. Captains and crews were all well known. Rafael asked whether individual fishermen ever did any private business in the town. Yes, they might if they had got their fingers on something salable, but nothing larger than a bottle or a box of cigars.

A dead end. He was no use as a detective. Well, but he was accepted as a leader and his orders were always eagerly obeyed. He could not help it, but it was so. Then shouldn't it be as easy to find a man who could smell out truth without being suspected as a man who would charge down on the police?

He chose for his agent Antón, the little fiery mulatto who had appointed himself bodyguard. He was always a source of news in the peaceful days before the boycott, more often behind a bar counter than in front of it — not serving or cadging a drink, but slipping in for a quick word or helping with the washing-up or reporting on business next door. He was one of those laborers, unskilled but versatile as a gypsy, who had returned from the Capital to his shack to find wife and children dead.

Antón almost at once discovered a bit of information which Rafael's diffident questions about fish marketing had not brought to light. The *Rosita,* a boat previously unknown, had called at Cabo Desierto on the same day that the new General Manager arrived. It had sold cheap on the quayside and had remained overnight. The fish was not fresh, and the skipper was suspected of having bought a job lot out at sea for sale to the hungry in Cabo Desierto.

If this was the boat which had brought the stranger and his boxes, it was easy to account for his transport. There were often empty trucks parked at night between the port offices and the quay, ready for business unaffected by the boycott such as lifting supplies to and from the market, the port and the Company Farm. So long as a vehicle was not parked bang in the middle of the main street the Company turned a blind eye. The weather was the same undercover or outside, and its transport could not possibly be stolen.

So it only needed a collaborator on shore to see that a truck with its ignition key in place was parked in a dark corner where no one would notice the driver. That part would fit Lorenzo very well. He had started in the garage, was always in and out of the workshops and above suspicion whatever his activities. Gonzalez might not have known anything. He and his police had no interest in routine movements of stores continuing for an hour or two after sunset.

Rafael himself had not the time to keep watch on the old field. Talk, all the unnecessary, resented talk, already allowed him too few hours for sleep. So again he delegated the job to Antón, asking him to see that Lorenzo or anyone else who turned up between dusk and dawn in the neighborhood of 32A was invited to explain his business. In a Christian manner, Rafael insisted; a knife might have to be shown but must not be used if there were no resistance. He found that, like any other commander, he had to tell his intelligence officer a good deal more than he wanted. However, the story was credible without any mention of Don Mateo; it was not essential to give an account of Chepe's movements after he had acquired his stick of gelignite.

Mr. Manager's hint about the Union could be correct, but that did not mean that one had to start touching one's cap to a helpless boss. Rafael resented those searching and inconvenient eyes when not answering them face to face. He was reluctant to admit that the explosives might be meant for the dam. It was indestructible. Sabotage of the water was an empty threat, covering some other dirty plan.

He did at least spend an hour inspecting the Charca, giving himself the excuse of an evening walk with Chepe. The pipeline from the old field to the head of the ravine seemed a possible objective, but what was the good of blowing it up when no water was coming down anyway? Then the downstream valve or the outlets or both? But how? He knew nothing of the placing of explosives and little of their effect.

He stood on top of the dam looking westwards at the sun resting on a copper Pacific. He felt that he was on the edge of the world and that beyond was nothing, friendly or hostile. This mood, common among all his friends and perhaps even to those heartless technicians in their gay

106

houses up on the ridge, was suddenly broken by a spurt of cold water on the back of his neck. Chepe jumped up laughing from the edge of the Charca with a water pistol in his hand.

"So that is what you learn in school!"

"I did not go today, papacito."

Chepe's small possessions varied from week to week according to the objects available for barter among his schoolfellows. Whatever he had, there was no need for anxiety. It had never occurred to him to steal.

"Then where did you get this weapon with which you dare to squirt your father?"

"The Man gave it to me."

"You must not accept presents from him."

"It was not a present. It was a bribe."

"That I can believe!" Rafael exclaimed indignantly. "What did he want you to do?"

"To go to school."

"Where did you meet him?"

"Up the hill. I was looking at the window of the shop."

In the executive suburb there was a small general store for the convenience of oil wives who had some chance of finding there whatever they had forgotten to buy in the town. It also sold toys attractive enough for children to point at them and cheap enough for mothers to drop them in the basket with the groceries.

"He asked me why I was not at school."

"And why weren't you?"

"Because I now know how to read and write."

"There are other things to learn besides reading and writing."

"That was what Don Mateo said."

"And then, Chepe?"

"He bought this gun for me if I would promise to go to school every day for a month."

"And you will do so?"

"Of course. I gave him my word."

Rafael did not approve, but could not help being proud of this son of his who innocently wandered everywhere and even managed to be on good terms with Gonzalez without involving his father.

The significance of the water pistol could not be missed. It was a reminder that the water supply was a pistol held at his head and that he must keep an eye on the Charca. The unfathomable mind of Don Mateo disquieted him; he was continually being disarmed.

Next day at dusk he set a picket of four men, two on top of the dam and two on the road below where they could rouse with a shout the nearest cottages. It did not matter that they could only be armed with pick handles. They were like soldier ants at the entrance to the nest. One signal from them, and reinforcements would swarm out to leave no more of any saboteur than broken flesh.

It was soon plain that sabotage would have been easy. A man could work all night on the Charca undisturbed. From Manuel Uriarte's house away at the end of the cultivated land came the occasional tinkle of a guitar if the breeze was from the north. Rafael had always imagined that behind the distant lighted windows was an austere scientist writing up his notes. There was never any other sound unless one counted the just perceptible rustle of nightly growth as leaf and stalk adjusted to the continual, minuscule crowding of fertility.

On the old field Rafael's other and more secret operation was quickly productive. At dawn on the third morning Antón came down with the news that his search had been successful.

"You have got Lorenzo?"

"No, Chief, he never appeared. But, better still, I have the explosives."

"Where were they?"

"Look! Sometimes a man such as Antón is needed. He is no mechanic, but when it comes to ropes and tackle and wedges and greasing a ramp, they listen to him. A hole boarded up — what had been there, I asked myself. What had I seen? I know the field better than you at work in your shop or Lorenzo who only drives along roads. What had I taken out of that hole which is boarded up?"

It was like the triumphant recital of a hunter come home with meat or of a *valiente* who had left his enemy dead. Rafael waited patiently until Antón, running short of breath, spread out his hands to invite him to repeat his question.

"So where were they?"

"You may well ask, Rafael! You told me to watch around 32A, but there was never any hole near it. Then I remembered a hole at 32, east of the derrick — a hole deep enough to hold a donkey where I myself pulled out the bailing engine more than six years ago. So I went to 32. Where the hole should be were some bits of old iron scattered so that no one should walk over it and hear his footsteps hollow. I kicked away the rubbish, and there was the cover of boards smeared with oil and gravel like the rest of the ground. And there beneath were the boxes!"

How then could Lorenzo have missed it? Rafael was sure from his behavior that he had been instructed where to find the cache, and with so simple a description he could not go wrong.

"But if Lorenzo was told it was at 32, son! He can read."

"He can't read what isn't there, Rafael. The number board has blown down. That was why Chepe didn't notice it."

It made sense. The numbering of the wells depended on when they were drilled. Number 32 had been an unprofitable wildcat. It stood among the fifties which had been drilled later and deeper. Number 32A, however, was where it ought to be, among the other thirties. Rafael could imagine how Lorenzo had started off in the right direction and then found only wells numbered in the fifties and no 32 at all. He naturally assumed that he had got lost in the dark maze of derricks and turned back to the more or less regular ranks of the thirties. There he found 32A all right, but no hole. So he was more lost than ever.

However, it was hard to see how the man from the fishing boat *Rosita,* a stranger whose face Chepe did not know, could be so familiar with the abandoned wells of the old field. A possible answer was that he had been given an accurate map of the route from 58, where his truck stopped, to 32 and so had found the boarded hole without any trouble.

Rafael woke the boy up and asked if he had seen the stranger looking at a map. Chepe, always eager for con-

versation as soon as he opened his eyes, demanded to know
what a map was. Rafael explained that it was like a scale
drawing in the carpenter's shop, but of places, not things.
Chepe thought very solemnly, put his forefinger to his
nose, hastily withdrew it, and came out with the information that the stranger had sometimes looked at a piece of
paper.

The worrying question was who had drawn the map.
Antón's answer to that was the hated Company, the assas-
sins capable of any iniquity. A month earlier Rafael's
answer would have been the same; but now at least he
could rule out the present boss who had warned him that
Chepe's toffee, as he called it, could be meant for the water.
And if Don Mateo had any reason to suspect where it was
he would never have employed his zombie of a chauffeur in
the dark but sent out a bold, no-nonsense search party.

"Leave it where it is until we have need of it!" he said.
"And not a word to anyone. There is a lot I do not understand."

"But we must have weapons, Chief!" Antón protested.
"Every man should have some of this stuff in his house. We
must have weapons. I tell you that even the Mayor's
revolver — the firing pin does not reach the cartridge."

"To hell with the Mayor's revolver!"

But Rafael's gloom faded away as he remembered the
incident. Antón had extracted the revolver from the municipal holster in full view of a delighted crowd while the
Mayor was waving his arms and trying to be heard.

"Not yet, friend," he said more gently. "This explosive
may not be so easy to use as you think. Perhaps Lorenzo
will show us when we are ready to make him talk."

SEVEN. There was no denying that the comfort of the club's shaded terrace was extraordinarily pleasant. A month earlier it would have been beyond any possible daydream that Mat should find himself, well paid, back in all the sensuous satisfactions of the tropics. Under his eyes in the comparative cool of the evening the tennis players twanged their little balls back and forth. Further away there were half a dozen couples on the nine-hole golf course.

Eighteen had been planned, with three long holes on top of the ridge, two devilish short ones and a long, downhill drive back to the valley. Every day at the bar someone would regret that Cabo Desierto had got the Sentinels on the ridge instead.

He had moved too far away from his compatriots. In war that had been unnoticeable. Even in a government office it had been disguised by the smoothness of routine for seven hours and thereafter the dispersal of colleagues into their private lives. But here — here the Company had made a home from home for its executives as well as its workers and, by God, he preferred the latter! He would rather have been sitting in the town café and knew it and hoped it didn't show. Probably not. His surface was as genial as anyone could wish. But even these expatriate suburbanites did in the end judge a man by his actions and not by his image. He knew they could not quite make him out. He appeared to be doing nothing too contentedly, and the nothing was not being done in the right places. As Gonzalez had pointed out, it was hard to tell where he would be and why he was there. The proper places in which to do nothing were the office or the club. Or at home with a whisky bottle. They'd have forgiven that.

He never felt his isolation when reality intervened. And what the hell did he mean by reality, Mat asked himself? Well, it included the men and the town and Garay and his son and even Captain Gonzalez; it did not quite include the games-players and their wives, though he admitted it would if the field were working flat out and at peace. Meanwhile their morale could safely be left to Bill Gateson, who was now strolling rather smugly across the lawn to the clubhouse after a masterly bit of umpiring. Gateson identified himself absolutely with the Company. He couldn't see that it had done anything wrong in detaining those husbands in the Capital; it had been just a tactful delay, not a grossly broken promise. His job and this green playground were reality for him. God Almighty! Reality was the bodies of seventeen women and five children painstakingly collected from their route and now buried in the new cemetery between high tidemark and the refuse of the shacks where they had lived.

He waved to Gateson to join him. As soon as he had made his cheerful gesture, one of the club waiters hurried over to his table and put in front of him a paper on a saucer as if it were a bill to sign. *Sr. Delgado wants to know where he may see you.* Mat pretended to sign it, writing: *Tonight. 11 p.m. Garden of my house.* Reality had intruded upon Decorum. A very proper marble relief for the Albert Hall, Mat thought — with fig-leafed waiter in the background who probably understood enough English to be able to pass on unguarded conversation to Delgado.

"Didn't see you this morning," Gateson said.

"No. I was at the school, Bill."

"What's wrong with it?"

"Nothing more than any other bloody school. I was arranging for school lunches. They have 'em in England. Why not here?"

"Who's going to pay for them?"

"The Three Sentinels. Meanwhile, a loan to the Mayor."

"You're getting no response, Mat."

"On the edge of it, I think. If I'm wrong I'll have to take up golf again."

"I didn't know you played."

"As a boy. It was a game then."

"What was your handicap?"

"I always remember that. At fifteen it was fifteen."

"Pretty good. What made you give it up?"

"Watching monkeys. Objectless activity."

"I say, that's a bit strong, isn't it?"

"Yes. Ever watched monkeys?"

"I can't say I have."

"They give you the woollies after a time."

The temptation to shake up Gateson was irresistible, but Mat knew he shouldn't do it. He turned on the charm, made room for the Chief Accountant and the Chemist, ordered more drinks, and produced a couple of good stories which Cabo Desierto could not possibly have heard before since they happened to be true. He was in top gear again, extending his momentary exhilaration to the lot of them.

A secret visit from Gil Delgado could be the beginning of the end — and then, with luck, a return to the golden days of Cabo Desierto when there was no need for any of these subtleties. If you wanted to talk to the General Manager you burst into his office with the drilling mud on your boots and got on with the business; or if you were a workers' delegate with a grievance you could go and raise hell with young Mat Darlow who would shout you down and fix it.

He walked home — another eccentricity which his subordinates hoped they were not expected to copy — and in by the gate of his house which now belonged to him alone. He had made Gonzalez remove that futile police guard altogether. Nothing could be said for it except the fish stew. Attracted by the nightly scent he had gone out for a plate, bringing a bottle with him. A very profitable hour had convinced him that all the police had ever planned was a safe line of retreat.

He warned Pepe that he would be sitting by the pool after dinner and officially not at home.

"You needn't come out to see if I want anything."

"I understand, Don Mateo. I will tell Amelia to see that your room has fresh flowers — and some champagne perhaps?"

"Business, friend, not fun! Two chairs and brandy and cigars on the pedestal of the boy."

"What boy?"

"The rim of the pool, I meant."

"You are too much alone, Don Mateo. Yet there are so many who are fond of you."

"It's a pity that my three ladies are so jealous."

"In England?"

"Up there on the ridge, Pepe."

At half past ten he sat back in his chair and waited. Funny mistake, that! He must have been imagining a place for the bronze boy so often that the statuette had become real. He wasn't looking forward to this interview with Delgado as much as he had. There was a smell of treachery. What an extraordinary word to think! Growing respect for that mad priest, Garay, evidently had something to do with it. Prejudice against Delgado was illogical and unjust — exactly the same feeling that made one despise the fellow who came over from the enemy in war, though his information might be beyond value and his motives impeccable.

Delgado came pacing round the house looking right and

left into the darkness like a lion distrustful of some scent on the wind. There was indeed a leonine touch about him, for he was a big, loose man with a brown mane — possibly the lightest hair among the workers of Cabo Desierto — and a sandy skin much the color of Mat's own. He sat down with a nod and without shaking hands.

"I give you my word that we are alone," Mat said.

"Don Mateo, I believe you are not a man to say something without a purpose."

"Brandy?"

"Thank you, no."

"Then I am compelled to drink alone, if you will excuse me. How is Don Rafael?"

"As always."

"That is why you have come by yourself?"

"He has a lot to do."

"More than ever now. What made him put a guard on the Charca?"

"Don't play with me! Because you advised it."

"I was not sure whether he had told you."

"We have no secrets from each other."

"But, all the same, you are here alone."

"And you, too! And do not forget it!"

"Don Gil, I am tired of telling people that one cannot negotiate with a dead man."

"Enough conversation! You said at the committee that no one would ever drive us from our homes. Were you speaking for the Company?"

"No."

"Then what am I doing here?"

"Sit down, man! I was speaking for myself."

"If you mean it, that's good enough for some of us."

"Don Gil, after a compliment like that I must insist that you take a brandy."

Delgado this time could not refuse. Mat observed that the slack, elastic line of his orator's mouth was equally well designed for wrapping round a fat cigar.

"I intend that any of you shall be able to rent his house whether he works for the Company or not. But you cannot call off the boycott on my word alone. The Company must formally agree."

"Who says we will call it off?"

"Nobody yet. There have to be votes in your committee and in London as well. I shall carry the day. Can you?"

Delgado sipped his brandy in silence and at last remarked that half the field would do whatever Rafael Garay said.

"What happens then?"

"Rafael is a man of peace, Don Mateo. He shows no mercy."

A paradox on the face of it! One never knew what would come out of these intelligent fellows whose only education was raw life. Mat saw what he meant. Britain and Hitler, for example. There was a limit to tolerance. Peace and mercy were two entirely different things. The more you believed in one, the less you could afford of the other.

"Then we shall be back at the beginning."

"That will depend on you and him. He believes what you tell him."

"And you don't?"

"That's as may be. Now that we know each other, what

was your game with the Charca? It's in your interest that
there should be no water for the land."

"They say that milk only flows from a contented cow."

"You've got one hell of a farmyard against you. Up here
between the ridges they do not trust you, Don Mateo.
They say you are paid to keep the boycott going. They say
they had to give up their policemen, and that women and
children dare not go out at night."

Annoying nonsense, but to be expected. It was difficult
for them to see sense in all his quiet building of bridges.
Yet libels and gossip were only flies to be brushed away.
They had no solidity like the knock-out punch which was
being prepared for Garay behind his back.

"And what does your waiter friend tell you that they say
about me in London?"

That at last got him a laugh. Delgado appreciated a good
thrust in his own style.

He saw him to the gate and went to bed contented.
Results were good for a first interview. It had not been
very cordial or conclusive but Delgado himself had asked
for it and his intention of proposing a return to work was
clear. The collapse of the boycott might even be without
violence if provocation were avoided. That, as Delgado had
said, could well depend on the friendship between Garay
and himself. A strong word, friendship. Better call it a lack
of bitterness.

After breakfast the managerial car was waiting for him
without the dutiful Lorenzo. He asked if he were ill. The
substitute driver supposed he was; at any rate Lorenzo had
not turned up for work. Mat thought no more of it and
gave orders that someone should go to his room and see if

he wanted anything. Lorenzo was probably suffering from a hangover — Cabo Desierto's occupational disease — being among the few workers with enough money to buy one. It was hard to imagine him ill; he had the sort of inhospitable body which germs bounced off.

Mat looked forward to telling Bill Gateson of his success. It would be a relief to share out even a little of the load. With all his faults, Bill was loyal and could deal discreetly with those libelous rumors up in the ghetto. He might also have some ideas — though sure to be too drastic — on how and where the intervention of the State could be valuable.

When the Field Manager came in, Mat was lounging in one of the deep chairs by the window of his office — an indication that there was no brisk morning business which demanded desk or telephone. Gateson was in a far from sunny mood. One could always tell. He was a handsome man with sculptured, rather Italianate features. If frustrated or out of his depth the straight mouth was inclined to become loose at the corners and the fine nose to droop over it — possibly because he tended to look down instead of facing the world with his usual, not unattractive touch of vanity.

Mat told him that there was at last a chance of a split in the boycott committee. They couldn't count on it, but should start planning for a three-cornered battle rather than the present solid opposition.

"It never looked less like it to me," Gateson said. "Do you know that black bastard Garay has put a guard on the Charca?"

"Yes. I practically told him to."

"You! You told him?"

"Why not? I don't think it had ever occurred to him that the dam could be emptied without his men being able to do anything about it."

"Who would do such a thing?"

"He asked me just that. I didn't tell him in so many words. The answer is the Union plus a trained saboteur with plenty of explosives and an hour or two to place them."

"But think of the loss of life there would be!"

A curious remark, that was. It did not fit at all with that first indignant snap of reaction when he heard that Mat was responsible for the guard.

There was no one in the communal lands overnight and the nearest houses were on rising ground. Even supposing that a pair of lovers were neatly tucked in between wheat and cane, they would have time to run. No saboteur could make any impression on the dam itself; he would have to go for the pipes, the downstream valve or the gates. That inevitably emptied the Charca, but not in one solid cataract. As an engineer, Gateson must see that. So why did he mention loss of life when he knew there would not be any?

Registering horror. Protecting himself from suspicion. God Almighty, of course he was! Gateson and Birenfield had been in it with the Union from the word go. And he had never suspected it for a moment. Well, set a trap and get the vile business over! One could stick a head out of the window and puke on the palm tree afterwards.

"The Union doesn't care about loss of life," he said. "And obviously they intended to put the blame on us."

"That was why you warned Garay?"

"Of course. If only there were some way of proving that the Company was not responsible!"

"I could suggest one, Mat."

"Well, go ahead," he answered cordially.

"I thought it best to make an up-to-date inventory of our explosives in case the store was broken into. That was before your arrival. I made Gonzalez check it and gave him two copies, one for himself and one for his chiefs."

"What's that got to do with it?"

"If the explosive used on the Charca was something we never used and hadn't got, it would let us out at any inquiry."

"For example?"

"Gelignite."

"I see. So you and Birenfield planned to break the boycott that way?"

"I don't understand."

"I think you do. At any rate, if you didn't plan it you made no effort to stop the Union."

"And why the hell should we? It's a gift!"

"To destroy all our cultivated land?"

"Starve 'em out. No nonsense about living without wages then!"

"It is not my policy to force men into desperation, Bill."

"No, I'll bet it isn't! Your way is to do damn-all except walk around with that supercilious smile on your face."

"Do you find much to do in the office yourself?"

"You know very well that I am working on plans for the new refinery."

He did indeed, for it had been his own suggestion. A futile task. London would certainly send out its own men when the time came. But Gateson's planning was sure to be elegant, and Henry Constantinides would find a use for it. He might well have it expensively printed with a colored jacket, put it, as it were, on his back and peddle it round the City. Gateson was a master of his trade in spite of his limitations; and after all he and Birenfield had a case, though their methods were nauseating. Courtesy must be preserved as long as possible.

"The smile — well, well!" Mat said with such humor as he could manage. "And I thought I was keeping up morale! It may be just that I have led a different sort of life from the rest of you."

"I'll say you have! We all know you were down and out when you grabbed this job."

"It's true there weren't any offers from Standard Oil or the Bank of England. But what has that to do with it? All the more incentive to get our oil flowing!"

"And a better incentive not to."

"How do you work that out, Bill?"

"Is it possible that one of the majors is paying you to keep the boycott alive?"

Certainly possible. At least three of the major oil companies were ready to buy before the boycott. The longer it lasted, the less the value of the field as a straightforward investment. So if the General Manager — this down and out fellow — could do with a fat credit in a Swiss bank account he had only to keep Cabo Desierto quietly heading towards insolvency.

A thousand to one that the jealous Gateson was himself responsible for this ingenious slander! Mat felt his forehead going red with shock and anger. It had not happened often enough in his life for him to have learned to control the flush. Anger was turning Gateson white. Guilt as well, no doubt. It would not be fear since he did not think his General Manager worth fearing.

It was time to put him out of pain — another sort of courtesy. He invited the beastly nakedness of power like some fool of an enemy commander who insisted on sacrificing his men for nothing. He had to be finished off so thoroughly that he would never be even a nuisance again.

"Bill, has it ever occurred to you that Cabo Desierto is on my side?"

"For God's sake, it bloody well isn't!"

"Not up here yet, but down in the town. You would know it if you ever talked to anyone outside this office and the club."

"And what do you mean by that?"

"I mean that I could take over the police tomorrow from Gonzalez if I didn't prefer to work through him. I mean that I have no need to get you sacked and produce a flaming row between Chairman and Managing Director. I have only to make known what you and Birenfield intended and let nature take its course."

"Are you threatening to have me murdered?"

"No, Bill. In fact I should put back a conspicuous police guard on your house to protect you, and see myself that it did. I should then dictate and collect signed statements from reliable citizens — which are so liable to be exaggerated in Latin countries. On the whole it seems likely that the Government would want you removed at once, of course to my great regret. Now, where is that gelignite?"

"I swear I don't know, Mat."

"But you know it is here."

"I think so. Birenfield gave me no details at all. He kept all the negotiations in his own hands."

"How far is Dave Gunner implicated?"

"You've met him. You know what he is. If anyone had tried to put him in the picture, he'd have stopped them before they could begin. He just told Birenfield to cooperate in every way with the Union and he would back him to the hilt."

"A fine lump of jelly to fall back on! Very well, I shall have the stuff removed in the way it came and Gonzalez will see that it is kept quiet."

"Gonzalez isn't in on this."

"No. Not altogether. But he knows the right address."

"Is there anything you want me to do?"

"No. Keep your trap shut and play tennis! There's no workable law of libel in this country, so I can't stop you saying what you like about me. But God help you if you make one move to interfere!"

When Gateson had gone, he gave himself five minutes to recover and then strolled into Pilar's office, needing her company but certain that his superior secretary would be with the Birenfield-Gateson party if she knew anything at all of the difference of opinion. She looked up from her desk with a half-smile and the usual neutrality of her large, brown eyes.

"Your driver, Lorenzo. There is a message for you that he is not at his house and nobody knows where he is."

"Gonzalez might know. I'll ask him."

"Shall I get him for you?"

"No. I'll go down to the port. There was a launch last

night which he might have taken. Did you tell Mr. Gateson
he was missing?"

"The message was for you, not him. Mr. Gateson walked
straight out."

"No pained smile for nurse?"

"Mr. Darlow, I have no idea what is the matter with
either of you, but you look as if you were being led out to
be shot."

"I've never seen anyone led out to be shot. Got a
mirror?"

She took a small, gold mirror from her bag and handed it
to him. Imperious. Pitying. And annoyed as well. He
couldn't imagine why she should be any of them.

"I can't see more than one eye. It's bloodshot and has
bags underneath. Orange washed with blue."

"Hold it further away!"

"Now I see what you mean. Game to the end. Gentlemen, the treasury is empty but I have served my country."

"And then you'd shake hands with the firing squad and
ask after their children."

"Any objection?"

"None at all. Do you remember asking me which side I
was on?"

"Stupid of me. Much too soon."

"Yes, but I nearly told you the truth. Which side would
you be on if you were descended from grandees of Spain
who had lived on the same estate for four hundred years?"

"Against the men, I suppose."

"Against everything! This silly, pretentious Company!
These cowardly crooks of politicians! There was nothing
then to take sides about."

"Well, if you look at it that way, there still isn't."

"You notice nothing!"

"Who noticed the carpet slippers?"

"For the gardeners, yes!"

"Always happier with the plain man," he answered uneasily.

"Because you're prejudiced. Because you think it's easier to find people to your taste at the bottom of society. You! A grandee yourself if there ever was one! Don't you see that is why you are trusted?"

"I have just found out that I am thoroughly disliked, Pilar."

"Jesus, man! Do you want all of us?"

It was the first time she had ever come out of her shell. If he'd got it right, she was trying to say that she was loyal to nothing but some quality she saw in him, putting her own name to it like most women. Just because he had always been able to handle local labor, it didn't make him some sort of aristocrat. All the same, he could now count on her approval, and that was going to be a lot pleasanter than staring at palm trees. There was no more need to sneak out with handwritten letters to Henry or to disguise his own moods with a lot of cheerful poppycock. What magnificent eyes the woman had when she was angry! He told himself that he had to be very careful or Miss Pilar would be ordering him about.

He asked her to radio an inquiry to the launch and to telephone Captain Gonzalez that he was needed. Her answering smile was slightly ironical. It was the first time that he had arranged a delicate and dangerous conversation — or what could be one — while she was in the next-door office. But he had good reason for not going down to the port, apart from his new trust in her. A valued employee of the Company was missing. The General Manager should be seen to be throwing his weight about, not slipping off downtown and giving the tennis players still another impression that he covered up idleness by an air of mystery.

Gonzalez arrived looking exceptionally well polished. There was no doubt that he felt more complimented when asked to call on the General Manager than he did when the Manager called on him. Odd, but understandable. He could think of himself as a valued staff officer rather than the little rat with whom one conspired in corners.

Yes, Lorenzo's disappearance had been reported and every effort was being made to find him. Mat was certain, however, that Gonzalez had not heard a word of the missing man until he entered the building. A few whispered words with the porter or with some friendly clerk casually met in a passage had then revealed why he was wanted and allowed him, a couple of minutes later, to assume a pose of having been occupied since dawn with the investigation.

Mat told him that the skipper of the launch had just replied that Lorenzo was not on board, and so it looked as if he had met with some accident.

"If you approve I will have a word with the boycott committee," he said. "We can count on their help with a search party."

"It may not be so easy, Don Mateo."

"You once told me he was faithful to his uniform. What exactly did you mean?"

Well, Lorenzo had no family. He lived in a company rooming house with three other employees who were foremen in the vehicle workshops. He had no known interests outside the Company and its cars. He was like a faithful dog, lost without a master.

"Pepe tells me that he considered he belonged to Birenfield. Could he have run away?"

"From you? Unthinkable!"

No, it was not. It could well be that he had failed to give to this masterless man a proper feeling of friendly security.

"We had little to say to each other and I did not let him drive enough."

"Where would he have run to?" Gonzalez asked.

"Suicide, perhaps. One never knows what is at work inside these closed men."

"He has not enough imagination, Don Mateo. For your safety it was my duty to know everything about Lorenzo. He does not drink to excess. He has not got a woman. He does not go fishing. We must ask ourselves who had anything against him."

This was a shock. It had never entered Mat's head that the man could be murdered. In prosperous times manslaughter, messy and in full view of a dozen witnesses, had not been uncommon. Secret assassination, however, was unheard-of and unnatural. He considered Gonzalez's question in silence. There was only one intrigue which could have involved Lorenzo.

"Does the Union have any permanent agent here, Captain?"

"Not so far as I know."

"Then a faithful dog could be useful. I have learned that before my arrival Birenfield had an understanding with the Union."

"For what I mentioned, Don Mateo? Impossible! Birenfield was correctness itself."

"Not arranging an accident for Garay, no. An attempt on the Charca."

"Outrageous!"

Gonzalez's indignation was unexpected. Mat had assumed that his only interest in the sabotage of the dam would be its effect on law and order; he should have had the opinion, normal to any bureaucrat, that a green world which produced content was of very minor importance compared to a black world which produced wealth. Yet the Captain genuinely considered the assassination of the land as a greater crime than that of Garay. Did he himself look forward to retirement in some flowered and fertile rat-hole? Or was it a surge of patriotism in the sense of love of his land and pride in the miracle performed on a waterless coast?

"You think Lorenzo was in it, Don Mateo?"

"I have no evidence at all. But the explosives are here. Someone must know where they are."

"What can I do? It is a nightmare to command police and be helpless."

"You have a sure way of communicating with the Union?"

"I have a contact."

"See him tomorrow! I will send you in the Company's plane to show you have my authority. You will warn those people to remove their gelignite as secretly as it came. And at once! Tell them that if the stuff gets into the hands of the committee I shall ask for a battalion and say why."

"Very gladly. And Lorenzo?"

"I suggest that you search the foreshore. Could we assume for the time being that he was accidentally drowned?"

"And if we find him with a hole in his head?"

"Then I can only pray that neither Garay nor Delgado was responsible. For your private information, dear Captain, there is a hope of peace."

"In that case it will be a clear case of suicide, Don Mateo."

EIGHT. Rafael had never intended that Lorenzo should be killed, never imagined any necessity for it now that the explosives had been found. Murder — or execution if one wanted a more decent name — was a blot upon the clean severity of the boycott. That troops and police would be killed if they fired was inevitable; oil workers too, of course. Rafael was prepared to give his own empty life and equally to smash the skull of anyone who tried to take it. But to slaughter in cold blood, no! He often told himself that he was like a warder in a prison. It was his duty to be vigilant and to punish; but so long as a man did not ask for trouble he should be treated decently and in a way that would not have offended Catalina.

Antón had sneaked off on his own to watch Lorenzo's movements without orders and without a word. Lorenzo was unimportant. There was enough to do without wasting time on him. But Antón was full of curiosity, a hungry curiosity like a puma on the trail of a wounded man.

"It was not in anger, Rafael. It was just that he was not to my taste."

"Man, if you are going to kill everyone who is not to your taste!"

"I tell you it was not in anger. I threw him down from behind and put the knife at his throat so that he dared not lift an arm. I asked him what he was doing in the old field. He said that he was taking a walk. So I laughed at him and told him we had found what he was looking for."

"There was no need to tell him."

"No. I saw that too late. But a man has his impulses. So then there was nothing for it but to cut his throat."

"It is as if something had deserted me, Antón."

"Don't worry, Chief! No one will ever know."

"Where is he?"

"Down with the stuff at 32. There is no better place."

"And the blood?"

"With all that oil and gravel one had only to turn the pancake upside down. Not God himself will ever see it."

But meanwhile, leaving God out of it, Cabo Desierto

bubbled and steamed with curiosity. Lorenzo was a familiar sight as he solemnly drove General Managers between the port and the ridges. In the absence of any motive or any known enemy, it was not automatically assumed that he had been murdered. He might have set off on the overland journey, or he might have gone for a swim and been eaten by a shark. A considerable body of opinion decided that he had remained hidden for a whole day in the Company's plane and flown off to the Capital with Gonzalez.

Under the circumstances it was easy for Rafael to shrug his shoulders. He was not in the least afraid of the law; there wasn't any and when again there would be, nothing could be proved. The only inquiry he dreaded was a direct question from Don Mateo. The lie he must answer mattered. He had exclaimed to Antón that something had deserted him. He couldn't put it into words, but, whatever it was, guilt had come in to take its place.

The affair of Antón and Lorenzo was best kept secret. The committee, however, must now be told of the windfall of gelignite and should consider what sort of weapons might be manufactured from it. There was a full meeting that evening called by Gil Delgado. Rafael was not sure what he particularly wanted to discuss and supposed it was his own fault for not grasping the point of Gil's explanation — a patter more voluble than usual about water and land and contracts.

They were all at the pavilion, all his comrades. Preliminary talk ran over the fate of Lorenzo and the reason why Gonzalez had been dispatched to the Capital. Presumably Don Mateo wanted reinforcements for the police, though it was hard to see why he should. The field was orderly and even if the police had been able to arrest an oil worker there had not been any offense to deserve it.

How well Gil spoke and how lucky it was that they had a leader who did not resent time spent in talking! Rafael listened intently at first and then with growing impatience as Gil went on about Europe and the Americas and Fascism and the Spanish Republic and said that if you refused to accept the decisions of the majority you were left with nothing but violence. A lecture on democracy, and what did it matter? The defense of Cabo Desierto was more important than all this hot air — defense which need not be bloody but just enough to show the Government that it would have to use overwhelming force against the workers and face possible revolution. That was real democracy for you! Loss of life? But what about those women in the new cemetery? This would be war and the killing of Lorenzo was murder. There was all the difference.

He woke up with a start from this woolgathering on hearing Gil declare that the Company was willing to give guarantees for the future. If a man paid his rent he could stay in Cabo Desierto as long as he liked and work at whatever he chose. Rafael waited for him to denounce the offer with a burst of indignation, to say that it was a bribe and to be refused. But Gil was recommending acceptance. He was asking them to call off the boycott and return to work.

Rafael was revolted by the man rather than his proposal. Evidently Gil, behind his back, had been negotiating with Don Mateo and had then sounded opinions privately. He jumped to his feet, shouting. He never knew that words could pour out of him like that and observed himself with astonishment — but only for a split second and without interruption of the flow. They had sworn revenge upon State and Company. They would farm their land and there was no one to stop them. They were utterly determined that the heartless pen-pushers in the Capital should for once be compelled to give way to the workers.

"All the world is against us," he cried. "We have no one but ourselves whom we can trust."

Gil was conciliatory. He begged Rafael to give his reasons, not to call names because opinions differed. They were all his friends and prepared to listen. There was no question of immediate surrender. First, they must see what they could get in writing. Meanwhile it would be foolish to answer Don Mateo with a flat refusal.

"So what will you answer?"

"That is for the committee, Rafael, not for me."

For the committee, yes. And Gil would succeed in muddling the clean issue for them until betrayal was signed and sealed.

"Enough words! You know I am not a talker. We settle it now by a show of hands."

He was voted down by eight to six. The six rose from the table together. Rafael, now calm, led them out and turned at the door.

"To hell with your majority! See whether you have a majority in the street! I hold the Sentinels, Gil Delgado. You cannot go back to work without us."

True enough. His own militant wing could not be beaten. They were able to double the pickets on the Sentinels, the refinery and the tank farm, and still patrol the streets if their opponents asked for trouble. But a permanent solution was not so simple. What about work in the fields and what about finance? Relief funds had fallen away but there was still one useful monthly transfer to the committee's account.

To think that he had been on the point of telling Delgado of the windfall of explosives! God forbid that he should ever have to use them against his friends, but it might come to that if they insisted on surrender. The thought appalled him. He blinked back tears and could not have said whether they were due to pity or rage.

His five companions tried to comfort him.

"Man, you look as if you had seen a ghost! Delgado and his blacklegs — they are not worth it. Here we stay and no oil ever!"

"And Don Mateo into the harbor!"

Rafael, turning his suppressed anger against the speaker, retorted that violence against the foreigners, any of them, was the surest way to bring in the army.

He avoided any singling out of the General Manager, unable to express the subtle relationship between them. Don Mateo, it was true, was ultimately responsible for this defeat; he had bided his time and split the committee. But there was no treachery in that. They had always been man against man, duty against duty. No, no harbor for him! If the worst came to the worst, he might be forcibly shipped off to the Capital; but it was hard to see what good that would do. Unless the Company stabbed him in the back — Gil said that he had bitter enemies — his plan for Cabo Desierto remained behind wherever he was.

Then and there, impassive and purposeful as cormorants standing on the edge of the breakwater, Rafael and his companions arranged for an action committee and a public meeting in the plaza which they would pack with men as relentless as themselves. At last he went home. At home was no treachery. He had Chepe and the memory of Catalina.

That boy! He would have tried to cook for his father if Rafael had not absolutely forbidden him to touch the paraffin stove. As it was, he had set out on the table bread, a raw onion and a jellied fish head in an unfamiliar plate. Rafael approached this delicate subject with caution, reluctant to spoil his son's small triumph.

"What have you eaten today, Chepe?"

"At the school! Very good! We had meat as we used to at home. But I could not bring you any. I had nothing to put it in."

"And this splendid head? Look, what whiskers!"

"They do not like whiskers. The man said that, by God, it was ugly but very fresh and I was to bring back the dish."

"What man?"

"In the hotel. At the back."

"You are not to ask for anything, Chepe. It is a question of our honor."

"I know that. I was passing and said good-evening and he called me into the kitchen. He said it was for me and my father with . . . with . . . something difficult. With the Compliments of the Management."

"He was very well brought up," Rafael said solemnly. "You could not refuse."

But even at home peace could not last. The pair had hardly sat down before Chepe asked:

"Papacito, what has happened to Lorenzo?"

"Who knows, Chepe?"

"Have you looked on the old field?"

"Lorenzo does not go there anymore," Rafael answered truthfully. "And I am too busy to bother with him. More busy than ever!"

"Busy with Don Mateo?"

"Nothing to do with him. We have other enemies now."

"Who, papacito?"

"Gil Delgado, for one."

"He is too large. I do not much mind if you kill him. He is not to my taste."

The echo of Antón was abominable. Not to my taste! Where would all this end?

"Chepe, one does not kill people because one cannot agree with them."

"What has Gil done?"

"He wants us to go back to work."

"Did you tell him we will not?"

"I did."

"Then that is the end of it."

It must be the committee, Chepe thought, that vague, exacting entity, which had made his father so preoccupied that he could not see the obvious. Of course Lorenzo had disappeared in the old field. Perhaps he had fallen down a hole; perhaps a rotten rig had collapsed on top of him in the night. Or he might have found what he was looking for, set a stick alight, and burned up as Don Mateo said might happen. Since papacito had no time, he himself would be useful and explore. Nobody would be about. He could call out Lorenzo's name as well as using his eyes.

All the next day Chepe wandered through the black forest of the old field, dead as if fossilization were silently spreading upwards through the rooted pipes. If not for the boycott there would have been a scattering of workers on odd jobs of salvage. As it was, he saw only headquarters staff — the water engineer and the chief electrician — who both ignored him. Weary of his search after a brave couple of hours, he lay down by the roadside in the shade of a tank and was awakened from his doze by a passing car. The car stopped and the Field Manager and Superintendent got out. Sr. Gateson nodded a response to his polite greeting as if he had trouble in seeing anything so small. Sr. Thorpe, whom he liked, asked him what he was doing up there.

"I am looking for Lorenzo."

"And why do you think he would be here, Chepe?"

"Because I cannot think where else he could be."

The answer was quite true and need not be expanded. He did not mention explosives. That was his own secret, shared only with his father and Don Mateo.

"Your father thinks so, too?" Gateson asked sharply.

Chepe disliked his voice and answered with the irresistible dignity of a child that his father was much too busy to bother.

"He has certainly got his hands full!" Thorpe replied. "Well, you might find Lorenzo, Chepe. Who knows? But take care of yourself and always look up at the rigs when you pass underneath. This place reminds me of a war ruin."

"Did you kill anyone in the war?"

"I did, Chepe."

"Why?"

"Because he would have killed me if I didn't."

"So that is right?"

"It depends what use we are to the world."

Chepe considered this statement. Since he greatly respected Sr. Thorpe, it had to be true, though it did not fit his experience. His mother had obviously been of use to the world but she was killed. He himself was no use at all as yet, but very much alive.

"I must ask Don Mateo," he said, though not really meaning to say it aloud.

"Are you ever alone with Don Mateo?" the Field Manager inquired.

"I have been, señor."

"And what do you do?"

"We talk."

"Does he put his arm round you?"

Sr. Thorpe exclaimed indignantly in English, but Sr. Gateson only smiled.

The question was none of his business and was not answered; one did not discuss with anyone at all episodes of tears and being comforted. Chepe excused himself politely. There seemed to be a quarrel beginning, but not like those of the men he knew. Sr. Thorpe was very angry, but Sr. Gateson still had his thin smile as if he had been at school much longer than Sr. Thorpe.

In the evening his father was uncommunicative. Chepe recounted his adventures, but was given no guidance on whether he had been useful or not; he hoped to be told that it was pointless to spend a second day as a detective. Since papacito was unwilling to be pestered about Lorenzo, he fell back on the Superintendent's laughing remark that he might find him. Tucked under his blanket, he decided that he should not give up so easily. The grown-up world was always insistent that one should finish what one had started instead of darting off like a hummingbird. Little blue hummingbird, his mother had said.

So again next day he toiled up to the old field, wandered aimlessly about, and called Lorenzo's name without any excited expectation that he might be answered. This duty finished, it was time to consider other duties. Absence from school had been in the back of his mind but had not entered any of his dialogues with himself. Now with no flower left to sip, alone and frustrated, the inevitable consequence of not going to school occurred to him. He had another duty. For a man of honor there could be no question. It could be performed at once, for the headquarters office was not far below him.

He stood before the porter, his large eyes shining just over the level of the desk, and asked to see Don Mateo. The porter laughed at him, which seemed to Chepe very absurd. Evidently the porter was not familiar with Don Mateo's character. Chepe pointed to the telephone — for in his experience he was seldom refused a reasonable request — and said:

"I am José-María Garay. Please have the goodness to call him on the thing."

The porter did so for the sake of a good story to tell. Chepe could hear a female voice reply. There was a short silence. Then the porter said Don Mateo would see him and led him to the elevator.

"It goes up," the porter explained, seeing the boy's reluctance to be caged.

"And it will go down?"

"You walk down."

There was a very long corridor and at the end of it a door where he was handed over to Pilar Alvarez, whom he knew by sight. He also knew of her distinguished family and did his best to give a little bow as he had been taught. He did not bow to the General Manager. He rubbed his hand on his trousers and held it out, for they were friends.

"I have come to give you back the water pistol, Don Mateo, because for two days I have not been to school."

"How was that, Chepe?"

"I was looking for Lorenzo in the old field."

"But why there?"

"He used to go up at night to find . . . to find what I had. You know."

"And do you think he found it?"

"Not when my father and I saw him there."

Mat did not immediately press his questions. There was no hurry, and he must not alarm the boy or send him away with an uneasy sense that he had been disloyal. Cabo Desierto was infected by quite enough disloyalty without spreading it to the innocent.

"And school, Chepe?"

"I can add numbers."

"How much is that and that and that?" Mat asked, dealing out three piles of small coins on his desk.

"Two and six . . . and four. Twelve, Don Mateo."

"Well done! Take them!"

"My father would not like it."

"He is very right. I am sorry. But it pleases me to give and I have no one to give to."

"You must get married and have a son, Don Mateo. Or are you too old?"

"That could be, Chepe."

"I saw Sr. Thorpe. He stopped to talk to me."

"For Sr. Thorpe we are all one family."

"He said it was all right to kill people who were no use."

Mat considered this. It was clear that Thorpe had been respectfully led into conversation, but he couldn't possibly have said anything of the sort.

"We are all of use, Chepe."

"Am I?" he asked — there was a note of puzzlement or anxiety.

"Of course. You will be a fine, brave person like your father and mother."

"Were Sr. Thorpe and that Sr. Gateson looking for Lorenzo, too?"

Careful now! Rafael might have put him up to that question. But Mat knew what in fact the pair had been doing: merely deciding where the new power plant should be when the refinery had covered the site of the present one.

"They had not a thought of Lorenzo, Chepe. Anyway your father has the explosives now."

"I don't think he has, Don Mateo. I could not show him the place."

"So you saw somebody hide it?"

"Yes. Under boards."

A hole and a cover of some sort. Mat remembered Pilar's conjecture — inferred from something said or not said by the women — that Birenfield visited the old field alone at night. There were boards all over the place and the man could presumably use a hammer and nails.

"I see. But what took Lorenzo there?"

"We think he was supposed to know where it was, but he didn't."

Another gap in the guesswork filled up. Birenfield was secretive, oversecretive, and rightly determined that the Company and its top executives should not be involved. But somebody in Cabo Desierto had to know where the explosives were hidden, and what better man than the silent, devoted Lorenzo?

This at last explained why Mrs. Gateson on that first night asked what he thought of Lorenzo. She expected that he had been told in London — by Dave Gunner? — that Lorenzo was a key man; her question was a hint, simply to give herself importance, that she was in the secret. Very possibly she had learned at one of those morning sessions in Mrs. Birenfield's bedroom how the General Manager proposed to break the boycott, and a good half of what Gateson knew might well have come to him through his wife rather than his boss.

"Thank you, Chepe. Tell Don Rafael that I am always ready to talk to him."

"I will. If we were not enemies, he would ask you to honor our house."

"We may not be enemies forever. Who knows?"

Pilar Alvarez gently took the boy as far as the head of the stairs. She returned in a mood that was far from gentle and wiped the genial smile off Mat's face.

"You send me crazy!"

"I've been told that before, Pilar."

"By every secretary you ever had, I should think."

"What's the matter now?"

"You build bridges everywhere except where you should."

"This isn't a bridge. It's a hobby."

"I know! But let it be thought you are using the son to spy on the father."

"That's just what I am trying to avoid, Pilar. I don't want to upset either of them."

"But there is gossip!"

"To hell with it!"

"You don't understand. You should see yourself when you talk to the boy. Have you ever looked at a woman as you look at him?"

"Damn it, Pilar, a woman is not a child!"

"For you, no! Never!"

He was quite unable to guess what had annoyed her. She was not a woman to mind Chepe being invited to the General Manager's office or escorting him to the stairs past popped-out, curious faces. It must be that she resented the preposterous touch of scandal. You could bet your life that Mrs. Gateson or some other idle, oil-fired female was at the bottom of it. Ignorant as well as idle surely? Or was there really some truth in the vicar–choir boy relationship which Sunday papers were so fond of? It was difficult to see where the fun came in.

Prejudice, more of class than color, was responsible. If Chepe had been one of those neat, emptily noisy children who played on the lawns of the executive ghetto and were educated by two imported governesses from nine to one, his choice of any one of them would have added to his popularity. Dear, kind Uncle Mat! Such a pity he never married! A lot of jealousy, of course, would have been stirred up because he had unaccountably preferred to toss a cricket ball at one rather than another, and accompanied by chatter that the mother of this paragon had played her cards very well. But no one would have found anything in the relationship which demanded explanation.

The bond between himself and Chepe was admittedly hard for them to understand. Indeed it couldn't be explained at all unless he gave away what had happened on that first night of his arrival. Without the key to it, this intimacy between the General Manager and the seven-year-old son of an obstinate, black carpenter was perhaps bound to be a little suspect up on the hill. Down below it wasn't. Rafael Garay himself, passionately proud of his son, seemed to consider the friendship partly comical, partly flattering, without any influence on the boycott one way or the other. Probably that view was shared by his comrades. They all knew Chepe when he took wings.

According to Pilar, his admiration for the boy was too transparent. And why not? He remembered that interview with Henry and Dave Gunner when he got the job, and how his triumph had been soured a little by the thought that there was no one dependent on him to share it or profit by it. Well, there never would be and meanwhile he would do what he pleased. When the chokes of the Three Sentinels

147

were opened again and few lives lost in the process or, likely enough, none at all, Gateson and his party would hesitate to invent any more Sunday paper conjectures even at the most private table of their country club.

NINE. Cabo Desierto, like a frontier village, observed the manning of positions on both sides of the line, each party ready for defense, neither willing to attack. Rafael Garay's mass meeting had the discipline of supreme self-confidence but did not overflow the plaza. Gil Delgado and the committee needed no meeting; their influence over the field spread by word of mouth. The minority in favor of no surrender was isolated though still admired.

As the field waited for a clash which did not come, anxiety was chiefly among the neutrals: the municipal council, the shopkeepers, the market, the clerks. In the taverns under the colonnade confident prophecies dried up. Their futility was too apparent. Action was for the General Manager alone. London had agreed to his proposals and only he could transmute paper into fact.

Except for the militants, men remained curiously aloof, disassociating themselves from both parties unless the issue was presented to them with all its oratory, threats and excitement. Work on the lands was more energetic than ever. For some it was a sullen refuge from the necessity to make up their minds; for others the burst of industry was a farewell, largely subconscious, to this gallant effort at living in the way of their ancestors. At dawn they picked up their tools cursing, but in the evening put them away with satisfaction. A man could see the result of what he had done. The older workers were very much aware of this. They remembered that when a well came in even the unskilled had known some sort of fulfillment.

As the Company plane swooped in from the sea, banked over the town and disappeared behind the refinery, Mat was sitting on the terrace of the little town hall, enjoying a municipal drink with the doctor and the Mayor and looking down on the length of the main street. All the faces between the plaza and the port turned upwards as if ranks of white, orange and brown flowers had suddenly opened in the sun. That was not normal. The Company plane was hardly worth a glance, and the only likely comment on its arrival was abuse of the blasted noise which disturbed a peaceful evening.

It was vivid proof of the tense mood of expectation. But expectation of what? Nothing much could be expected of the return of Captain Gonzalez, and it was most unlikely that the Government, holding its collective breath like Cabo Desierto, was about to take any action whatever. Expectation was presumably for some impossible link — bomb or letter or a winged President of the Republic — between the unlimited sky and Rafael Garay stubbornly on the ground.

The Mayor, like most of his fellow citizens, at once turned for distraction to a minor problem.

"Legally we should be holding the elections," he complained. "But what am I to do till this is over?"

"It's of no importance. You will be returned unopposed."

"But my council, Don Mateo!"

"I will get Gonzalez to certify a state of emergency. Elections can't be held."

"Is that constitutional?"

Little that any of them were doing was strictly constitutional. But the Mayor's question was not, Mat decided, as absurd as it seemed. When a man had authority without power, he was sensitive on the point of where it came from. That was about all one could say for democracy, and it was quite a lot.

"Policemen and doctors cannot be argued with," Dr. Solano remarked. "When we say it's an emergency, it is."

"Gonzalez does nothing but knows everything," the Mayor grumbled.

"Except his own men," Solano added.

Mat gave him a quick glance. It was plain that Luis Solano knew the reason why the women bolted in secret from their shacks and had kept silent, common sense backing up the Hippocratic oath. His brown eyes were calm and noncommittal as usual, but there was a thin smile under the moustache. Curious that so many Latin American doctors should grow moustaches! Perhaps it was as far as they dared to move from the dignified medical beards of their fathers; perhaps a moustache helped to stiffen an upper lip too sensitive to pity.

"Why don't you both come up the hill and dine with me?" Mat asked.

"Now that would delight me. Your society and the cooking of Amelia!" the Mayor exclaimed. "But papers await my signature. My evening is not my own. For me the office, the marital couch and in the morning back to work!"

It was the marital couch which mattered and all Cabo Desierto knew it, though no one would have punctured the mayoral myth of pressure of business. The dear old boy, conforming to the tradition of comic opera, had been caught with his pants down — literally, it was said — in the back room of his wife's pretty dressmaker. Thereafter if he did not go straight home he was accused, with formidable ululations, of making a fool of himself again. The Mayoress would have telephoned Amelia to see if he were really at Don Mateo's house — an unbearable humiliation for the elected head of the community.

Mat and Luis Solano stayed with him until the lights came on in the plaza, listened for a full ten minutes to his reluctant good-byes, and drove up to the General Manager's house where Mat suggested that they should wait in the garden.

"I did not warn Amelia and, since it's you, she'll insist on at least an hour's cooking."

"This is magnificent," Solano said, standing at the west window.

A full moon revealed Mat's imagined world curve more desolately than the sun, and a breeze off the sea carried faint and continuous moaning of surf as if the spinning of the earth were audible.

"Yes, but it makes me feel alone in space."

"You don't like that?"

"Too near reality. It's a pity about the Mayor."

"He's so ashamed of himself that he can't see he has doubled his popularity."

"Natural enough if he hasn't any peace at home!"

"It will wear off. It's only that she is feeling like your space traveler — and noise is the remedy."

Pepe with a lamp and bottles led them down through the terraces to the pool and announced before retiring that dinner would be in half an hour which it certainly would not.

"So you knew why the women set off on their march?" Mat asked.

"Yes. But I was not sure that you did."

"I have wondered whether to tell Garay. It was the State which sent those blasted police."

"But it was the Company which delayed returning the men. Let it stay at that and don't complicate things! You must never allow Garay to feel like a cornered animal."

Darkness outside the ring of light was absolute. The land, dense and comfortable under its green growth, silenced the Pacific and shut off the moon.

"You weren't afraid at first to be alone here?" the doctor asked.

"No, Luis. In a sense I had come home."

"The best move you ever made was to dismiss the police guard. It lowered the temperature."

"I had nothing to lose. It wasn't the same for others with wives and children. They felt that police were better than darkness. Jane Thorpe warned me."

"They have never quite forgiven you. I don't want to tell you the latest libel, but you ought to know it."

"I do know it. The bronze boy and all that."

"Bronze?"

"Anything but black iron or pale stone. I could have found his color among my timbers once."

"Mateo, you had a happy childhood."

"I did — after my father and I were left alone."

"Your mother died young?"

"No. Gave us hell and then cleared out."

"So that is why you never married!"

"Is it? That's never occurred to me. There was always a new job. Or war. Or something. I don't know where my life has gone. But I've enjoyed myself. Would you believe that I have never taken a sleeping pill or a tranquilizer?"

"That's only because you use alcohol very skillfully. What about women?"

"I have always been able to give satisfaction."

"To give?"

"That's more than half the fun of it."

"You must have created a good deal of unhappiness, Mateo."

"Why?"

"Haven't women loved you?"

"I suppose so. Perhaps I never stopped long enough to find out. They get desperate so easily."

"I think you want to give but only on condition that you are not possessed."

"Christ, no! I possess myself. Stop trying to analyze me and drink up, Luis! You're here to sew the bits back on to casualties."

"And also to give advice when I know the facts."

"Well?"

"I recommend an affair with Pilar."

"Pilar? I'm not going to be run by Pilar!"

"She might want to give, too. You aren't the only one."

"Bloody charity! I'll be sixty before I know it."

"With nothing."

"With the devil of a lot, my lad, if I can get the Three Sentinels flowing."

"I didn't mean money."

"Nor did I. Don't you count memories, Luis?"

"Yes, if you have somebody of your own to tell them to."

"If I didn't know Pilar would rather die first, I'd say she had put you up to this."

"You don't realize how fond of you we are, Mateo. About half the town has put me up to this."

What islands we all were! A man saw only the merest outline of the picture his society made of him. Mat knew that he was liked, yes, but not to such an extent that Cabo Desierto would lovingly plan for his private future like a bevy of retired midwives. Warmth flowed round him; it was embarrassing and could affect his judgment. And a lot of nonsense that was! His judgment had been affected by warmth, his own and theirs, since he landed on the quay.

"Let's go up and bully Amelia," he suggested. "She's always flattered by a head poking round the kitchen door even when she wants to throw something at it."

The evening spread out into a lake of restfulness. Amelia surpassed herself. Luis Solano laid off the personal questions and entertained him with stories of his compatriots and their initial distrust of foreign doctors — which turned quickly to such exaggerated confidence that they preferred to be treated at the Company's miniature hospital and refused to be flown to the Capital unless Solano protested his absolute ignorance.

He thought that typically British, but Mat was sure he was wrong. It was just another example of the isolation of Cabo Desierto, always on the defensive and proud of itself. Luis was a fearless and admirable general practitioner, but that was not the point. He belonged to them. He, too, was a prisoner between the ocean and the Andes.

Next morning Mat had some difficulty in meeting those aristocratic eyes of Pilar, but was in genial form for Gonzalez, who came up to headquarters to report on his journey to the Capital. The captain was unusually straightforward. For once he had been given definite instructions and was sure of powerful backing. He had seen his contact in the Union and delivered Mat's ultimatum that the explosives must be removed. It was accepted — with some relief, Gonzalez thought — but there were still difficulties. The cache was on the old field and only two people knew exactly where: Lorenzo and the expert who was to undertake the demolition of the Charca's gates.

"Did they know Lorenzo has disappeared?"

"No. I reported it to police headquarters as a matter of routine of no special importance. A piece of paper filed away until I add to the dossier."

"Since you left I have it from a reliable source that Lorenzo somehow misunderstood instructions and could not find the right place."

"It does not matter. They will send the man who hid the explosives to collect them. All he needs is a truck."

"How will he come?"

"By fishing boat. That's how he brought them in."

"Where did they get this fellow from?"

"They did not tell me and I could not ask too many questions. But there is a discreet surveillance of visitors to the Union office, and I felt sure I could identify him from the files."

Gonzalez pulled out his notebook.

"Here, Don Mateo, we have him without any ifs or perhapses. Inocencio Velez García. Age forty-one. Born Barcelona. Anarchist and *dinamitero*. Republican refugee. Employed during the war by British agents in Valparaiso. Believed to have been secretly trained by them. In hospital 1949 for extraction of three machine-pistol bullets. Claimed he had no enemies and must have been mistaken for someone else. Communist agents suspected. 1952 arrested for bank robbery. Unshakable alibi and case dismissed. Witnesses bought by funds of unknown origin. Present employment: watch repairer. Known in his own circles as El Vicario."

"Sounds as if he gave good value for money," Mat said. "Why should he agree to come and collect the stuff? If police want a chat with him they have only to catch him unloading."

"The property of the Union, not his."

"And they are above the law?"

"Provided they have a good enough story. Besides that, Don Mateo, I have assured them in your name that we do not want to know how their property got there or what it was for."

All satisfactory so far as it went. Mat was thankful that he had persuaded Rafael Garay to post the guard on the Charca. That was checkmate if there were any attempt at a double cross by the Union or their expert from Barcelona.

Nowhere else, however, was there any simplicity. The foreground of the picture was unfinished, blank as the face of the Cordillera. He had little doubt that Lorenzo had been murdered. The Union was the likely culprit. On the other hand Gonzalez was sure they knew nothing, and he was not easily fooled. Yet Lorenzo's disappearance must somehow be connected with the explosives.

"What's your plan when the fishing boat arrives?" he asked Gonzalez. "I've been the hell of a lot of things, but never a gunrunner in or out."

"We should not show ourselves at all. The Company and the police must not be involved. When the boxes are safely on board I will check the contents and get the boat away immediately."

"I think we should promise Inocencio something in cash over and above the Union rate for the job. Have you any idea how much of it there is?"

"A hundred and fifty kilos, they said — plus his own refinements."

"Refinements. Yes. Your watch repairer would have been safely away by the time that little lot went up."

"Can your reliable source help us any more?"

"No," Mat replied rather too bluntly.

"It is true that at that age the more one interrogates the less sense one gets."

Mat was amused by the acute and accurate guess, but did not comment on it. Police captains, in his experience, could never resist showing off their cunning once they had been admitted to intimacy.

"Do you think it safe to question Delgado?" he asked. "He genuinely wants peace."

"He wants his chance and has taken it."

"You don't approve?"

"Me? I am a shadow, Don Mateo, careful to whose feet I attach myself. There are men such as yourself and Garay who do not seek power but have it. There are politicians like Delgado who want it for its own sake. He is a crook and in your hands."

"A good reason for telling the truth?"

"In my business, none better."

It was always a relief to be able to talk openly with Gil Delgado. Daily he paced in and out of headquarters, belly swinging, ready to be ingratiating with anyone but Gateson. Mat agreed with Gonzalez's reading of him. His game was to emerge as the leader who had brought peace and so to become the unchallengeable representative of the Cabo Desierto workers. That could well lead to a position of national importance; in Delgado there was another Dave Gunner on the way up. He was quite ruthless enough to deal with Lorenzo without any sense of guilt, but it was

159

hard to see how that uniformed dummy could ever have been an obstacle to his plans.

Mat received him in the conference room rather than his office, emphasizing that they talked as equal to equal with a common interest. He had noticed that the padded chairs and polished table had an excellent effect on Delgado, who already felt himself the politician among lawyers and engineers. Sherry of course improved his manners, but not so much as the decanter and cut glasses. And very rightly!

In the event of a clash what arms had Rafael Garay? Very few, Delgado replied, but no one should underrate iron bars and knives. Explosives? Yes, a few dozen sticks of dynamite and some detonators, but no plans for using them beyond poking them into scraps of pipe. Had Rafael any secret stock? None at all, Delgado answered positively; he would have known about it.

"Rafael will never attack his comrades or you, Don Mateo, provided we go slow. But give him an excuse to fight and he will take it."

That was good advice and sincere. In the easy atmosphere Mat risked the direct question.

"Have you any idea what could have happened to Lorenzo, Don Gil?"

"I suspect that he knew too much for his health. He was always with Birenfield — the pair of them in enough mud to drown a cat."

"It could be Garay?"

"Not for a moment! Rafael is a Quixote. Violent, yes, but more Christian than the Christians."

"All the same, rumor has it that he fired those two shots at Birenfield."

"He did, but not to kill."

"And you still think I can get the men back to work without bloodshed?"

"Of course! They'll get tired of it, man. All this for some women and children, which was only an accident!"

So that was now Delgado's attitude! To Mat, the Company's cheating on their men was still unforgivable; to refrain from saying what he thought had needed more self-control than any of his guarded moves to undo the damage. Humanity — one despaired of it! Delgado's "only an accident" was as damnable as Dave Gunner's "only foreigners." Garay and his party were utterly wrong-headed, and it was not at all more Christian than Christians to allow resentment and vengeance to overcome common sense; but for themselves there was nothing to be gained except a poor living off the land. That was to be respected.

The days which followed were the worst that Cabo Desierto had given him. When the boycott committee accepted his proposals, congratulations had poured in from London and the Capital, but now the high hopes had led to nothing. Only force could shift Rafael Garay and his toughs from the key installations of the field and the Three Sentinels. Delgado was probably right in maintaining that the militants would dwindle away, but meanwhile he was helpless.

Disappointment was at its most bitter on the field. He was blamed for not calling in the army. Gateson had let slip the plan to empty the Charca and whispered that Mat himself had prevented it. Even Ray Thorpe was impatient and for the first time in favor of machine guns. None of them could honestly say "I told you so," but the four words haunted his loneliness as if they had.

It was with a feeling of holiday that he joined Gonzalez at the port to observe the arrival of the *Rosita* and that watch-repairing El Vicario. The operation was of minor importance compared to starting the flow of the Three Sentinels down to the sea, but at least provided an illusion of action. At four in the afternoon he had seen from his ocean grandstand of a window a black speck on the horizon which had to be the fishing boat. When he reached the customs shed she was in sight at sea level, and ten minutes later the thudding of the Diesel could be heard. So silent was the town that he could detect the beat echoing back from the sharp slope of the ridge. Human beings were sweating out the last hour of siesta; their stillness emphasized the other interminable silence of the field and its machinery.

Rosita rounded the breakwater with two alarming rolls, like a drunken sailor keeping balance and a purposeful course in spite of his legs, and tied up close under the customs shed, her deck just below the level of the quay. Three men began to discharge her boxes of fish. It was not a big catch, but seemed to be very fresh and of a quality better suited to the Capital than to Cabo Desierto. Meanwhile the master walked into the port offices to report his arrival and telephone the buyers in the market.

Watching through the window of Gonzalez's office, Mat remarked:

"A retired naval officer who deliberately hasn't shaved for two days?"

"Possibly. But two of the crew must be genuine fisher-men. Last time the fish was bought, not caught, and they hadn't enough ice."

"Which is the expert?"

"He must be the little one."

That was obvious when one looked closely at the three men sitting on the edge of the empty fish hold. Though the slenderness of the Spaniard, the color of his skin and his bared, muscular arms were not very different from those of his mestizo companions, he lacked their softness of outline. He was tense rather than thin all the way from forehead to feet.

"You had better go back now, Don Mateo, before the buyers arrive."

Certainly it would be wise. If things went badly wrong and the General Manager was down at the port for no apparent reason, everyone would assume that he was impli-cated.

"How long will El Vicario take?"

"He will go up after dark and should be back in an hour."

"They'll be seen loading the boxes on board."

"It doesn't matter. With all four at work it should not take them more than three minutes — then cast off and away!"

"What will you say the boxes are, if asked?"

"Ice from the market in their own containers. That's what they told me and why should I bother?"

"A damned unlikely story!"

"Of course. So people will assume it is one of my rackets and settle for that."

"Let me know as soon as *Rosita* is clear! I shall be at my house."

Mat drove back to headquarters and signed a mass of correspondence, none of which had anything to do with oil or the men who refused to handle it. Law, houses, land — he might as well, he thought, have been a smart estate agent flogging properties for retirement. Sun-drenched plot with uninterrupted views over the Pacific. Money back if it rains more than once a year. Company's water, provided organized labor doesn't blow it up.

"Pilar, do you consider all your police to be crooks?"

"You know they are."

"Can you think of any racket that Gonzalez could possibly be in?"

"He hasn't much opportunity at Cabo Desierto, but I suppose we could frame him if we have to."

Not much of grandee ethics in that! Well, she must be excused for the sake of the unquestioning loyalty in the "we." He felt a sudden access of pity for poor, cynical Gonzalez who saw so clearly that in any dubious intrigue he could be left holding the baby. The captain's unreserved trust, which had often seemed a mere frightened choice of the right protector, was really a great compliment.

He went home after dark and relaxed over his long evening drinks on the veranda where he was within easy reach of the telephone. It refused to ring before, during or after dinner. Several times he left the table and went out into the darkness to look for *Rosita*'s triangle of lights which should be visible when she was a mile or so out from Cabo Desierto.

Pepe came in to clear away the coffee bearing a message

from Amelia that she hoped there was nothing wrong with the steak of barracuda in his favorite *salsa verde*.

"I told her that your mind was on business and you were always looking out of the window," Pepe said. "But she had to know."

Business, yes. No feeling of holiday now. This secret removal of the gelignite and its temptations was vital to success.

At last he was sure that he saw *Rosita*, though there were no points of red and green. The white masthead light vanished as soon as spotted — only the phosphorescence, perhaps, of some great tail flicking the water. Soon afterwards Gonzalez called to say that their friend was not yet back. Underlying his discretion there seemed to be a note of worry.

It was nearly midnight when Gonzalez himself came up to the house with the news that the truck was back, empty, in the same obscure lane from which it had been taken. He could not understand it. Nothing should have gone wrong.

Inocencio had lived up to his name. He drifted off about seven o'clock, went to the fishing crews' usual tavern for a drink and a snack, walked up the main street in pretended search of amusement and drifted down again to the port. There Gonzalez intercepted him and discreetly slipped him the extra payment which had been gratefully received. The man appeared trustworthy and confident.

After leaving Gonzalez he walked past the parked truck without looking at it and then, as if struck by its convenience, turned back into the darkness between the truck and a blank wall where he had a leisurely pee. That finished without any disturbance or any passerby, he jumped straight into the cab of the truck and was away. A police patrol concealed near the road junction between the ridges reported that he had driven through to the old field. That was all Gonzalez needed to know and he had withdrawn the patrol.

"What have you done with the truck?"

"Put it in with my police vehicles and been all over it."

"Any sign of a struggle?"

"None yet. All I can tell you so far is that he never loaded the explosives. There are oil and gravel on the floor of the truck, but no marks of boxes."

"And the boat?"

"Still in port. The master is protesting about staying overnight, but I have told him that he must."

Mat gave orders that in the morning the old field had to be thoroughly searched by the police. Secrecy could no longer be preserved, for somebody must know exactly what they were seeking. That somebody might be an unexpected Union agent or Rafael Garay or even Gateson. But there was an excellent excuse for the rest of Cabo Desierto. The Company and the police were looking for the body of Lorenzo.

Under some boards. That was the only clue. Ray Thorpe, let into the secret of the real object of the search, was sure that he had never ordered any hole to be boarded over; but anyone could have made a quick, strong job of it with duckboards or planks from shed floors and drilling platforms. He would have a record of any sizable object or engine which had been removed during the actual closing down of the field. Before that, when the field had been in full production, swappings and shiftings of machinery had been of almost weekly occurrence. His diary might be helpful and he would look, but he would probably come up with scores of possible holes.

Without any rain to wear away the ground, the year-old footmarks of Thorpe's gangs remained much as they had been made. They could be deep in oily sand or stand out on rock as if they had been painted black or leave a vaguely foot-shaped mat of gravel and oil. There were impressions of a child's foot confirming the presence of Chepe. He seemed to have been accompanied by an adult and to have wandered about among the ranks of the thirties. That this was the right quarter was corroborated by prints of Lorenzo's boots, the soles of which were known and entirely different from the rubber boots or canvas shoes of the oil workers. There were signs that he had once walked from the road into the fifties. Chepe, too, had once gone some way in that direction. But there was no doubt at all that their main search had been in and around the thirties.

Inocencio Velez García, alias El Vicario, had disappeared as completely as Lorenzo. To Mat it seemed highly probable that he was at large and planning to get clear of Cabo Desierto by the overland route for good reasons of his own. He was the sort of wiry, desertworthy fellow who would take the risk, especially if he had a partner ready to ride out from the Capital to meet him with food and water. He might of course have been murdered, but it would be a more chancy business to deal with him than with Lorenzo. As a freelance *dinamitero* who had managed to reach the age of forty-one he was likely to have escaped more bullets than

the three which hit him and to have left the odd corpse behind in the process.

There was nothing for it but to give up the search. The
master of *Rosita* refused to wait any longer. His orders to
be away before dawn were precise and his pay depended on
obeying. All he knew was that he had to land a passenger
and take him off again with a load of boxes during the
night. Mat damned his employers for being overdiscreet.
One could see their point. If *Rosita* ever came under suspicion, any investigation would soon bring to light who had
twice chartered her and why.

TEN. From the garden of the Farm Manager's house the black oil field was out of sight. The landscape visible through a windbreak of tall eucalyptus was divided as neatly as any flag into blue ocean, green farmland, yellow mountain. The only reminder that Industry existed, silent and on the defensive, was the cluster of tanks beyond the port, their steel tops flashing like round shields in the sun.

Rafael was a frequent visitor, quick to learn and eager to

ask the questions of the ignorant which to Manuel Uriarte often seemed more penetrating — if one really tried to give an honest answer — than those of experienced farmers. The agronomist could not approve his obstinacy but understood it, being himself full of compassion towards his fellows, most of whom would all their lives be deprived of his own utter satisfaction with his work.

"You are not reasonable, Rafael."

"This is our home. And, thanks to you, we can live without wages."

That to Rafael was the point upon which there could be no surrender. Revenge upon the Company, yes — but justified by his nebulous vision of a peaceful return to what men were meant to do. In Cabo Desierto could be a society of quiet growth, of creation in emptiness to fill the other emptiness left behind by Catalina. A majority did not agree with him. Well, but in the end it must. Here could be happiness, a living lesson of what would happen if one rejected companies and treachery and cowardice. That only Capitalism or the State could have financed Uriarte's artificial paradise he understood, but there was no reason why the workers should not take it over.

"The Company has promised that anyone who wants to live off the land may do so."

"The Company is dead. We have killed it as it killed our women."

"There is always Don Mateo."

"True, there is Don Mateo. But this is a question of principle."

One single man stood in his way. The Company was powerless and the State afraid. That outside world, against which Gil used to warn him, could be defied, for no one else was prepared to use armed force if the government was doubtful. Don Mateo had won the first round but could not win the next. Rafael had no resentment against that single man, that courteous single man, only against Gil Delgado who had sold out for the sake of his own importance.

"Reasonable!" Rafael spat the word. "To you Delgado is reasonable!"

"Yes, Rafael, I think he is."

"And what have you to say to treachery?"

"Man, I am talking of his policy, not his character."

"An absurdity! What a man is and what he does are the same."

"But not in politics, Rafael."

"This is not politics. This is war."

"All wars end in peace some time."

"But that is all I ask. Peace and no oil!"

Down the black bar of the road which separated the farm from desolation something white glided in and out of sight, changing rapidly from a determined gull to a figure bent over the handlebars of a bicycle and pedaling fast through the heat of the late afternoon.

"Someone for you," Uriarte said.

"Why for me?"

"Here we grow things. There is nothing so important that it cannot wait for the sun to pass."

Antón, soaked in sweat, jumped off his borrowed bicycle, greeted Uriarte, and panted to Rafael that *Rosita* was in port again.

"What have you done?"

"Set a watch to see what she unloads. The skipper does not look to me like a fisherman."

"A favor, Don Manuel! Would you drive us to the town?"

"So much hurry for fish?"

"For the safety of the Charca," Rafael replied, certain that Manuel Uriarte could be trusted with some of the truth. "We believe this boat may carry an expert to blow it up. On her first voyage she brought the explosives."

"Don Mateo would never allow it."

"To hell with Don Mateo! I think he knows and does not know. It could be someone in London or the Union or Gonzalez or any other bastard without shame. You and I do not see eye to eye, Don Manuel, but neither of us will let all this go back to desert."

"A fairy story! But it costs nothing to drive you in. Throw your bicycle in the back, Antón!"

Uriarte dropped them at the market. There Rafael quickly confirmed that *Rosita* had really brought fish, though hardly enough to make a call worthwhile. He had not time to trail or question the crew, which anyway would only arouse suspicion. Since nothing was certain, the right game was to go up to well 32 in the dusk, hide, and await developments.

Rafael collected three of his best men from the guard on the Sentinels, skirted the south end of the golf course in the last of the light, and then climbed the second ridge into the old field. His plan was to post the three along the route from 58 to 32 with orders to watch but to take no action unless he himself shouted to them. Meanwhile he and Antón would remain hidden within a few yards of 32. He could not tell whether the unknown visitor meant to bring in more explosives — in which case they would be gratefully received — or to collect what he needed for an attempt on the Charca; but by the time he had lifted the boards and started work his intentions would be obvious.

The first essential task for Rafael and Antón was to remove the body of Lorenzo — a private affair which there was no reason for anyone else to observe. They had no chance to do it. The party was still picking its way in darkness between 58 and 32 when a truck was heard crawling up the approach road without lights. Rafael, flustered by the unexpected speed of the enemy's arrival, quickly posted his men where they were and himself ran forward with Antón to 32 where they vanished into the complex blacknesses and lay still. It occurred to Rafael that in the hurry he might have underrated the sort of emissary who would arrive on *Rosita*. He and Antón had only their knives and the Mayor's revolver with the dubious firing pin. Their three comrades were too far away to support them.

The truck stopped. They would have had plenty of time to deal with Lorenzo. It was a good quarter of an hour before the driver appeared. How he had come and for how long he had observed his objective was a mystery. They had not heard a sound or seen any movement until the figure materialized from the night already standing by the boarded hole. He stood quite still, listening. Rafael could have sworn that he was smelling the air, too, and that their presence must be detected by a man whose professional wariness was so evident. He himself was lying between two balks of timber with the fallen number board over him to hide the paleness of shirt and trousers. Antón's position was more free. He was curled up under the derrick and indistinguishable from the wellhead.

Satisfied that he was alone, the saboteur began to clear away the junk and scraps of metal over the boards; and even this he did carefully with the least possible noise. He raised the cover, shone his torch inside the hole, and with a single flow of movement plunged into a patch of thicker darkness. There was just enough starlight to distinguish his outline and an outstretched arm, menacing as a snake, with an automatic pistol at the end of it. Rafael did not think that Antón would be able to see him at all, and was thankful. Though Antón's orders were that the man should be taken alive if at all possible, one could never be sure of him. He was quite capable of impulsively trying a shot and either giving away his position by the click of the misfire or missing.

There was silence except for the faint whines and rattles of the wind among the rigs. Patience came naturally to Rafael, and patience had a good chance of being the deciding factor in the end. The enemy should be tackled while his hands were occupied in carrying boxes, either there at 32 or at the truck or perhaps on the way to it. He waited. Antón would not find it so easy. Twice he saw him change to a more comfortable position, undulating round the wellhead like a cat and quite invisible through the dark, vertical stripes of the derrick to anyone who did not know he was there.

At last the stranger stood up boldly and returned to the hole. He dragged up the body of Lorenzo, laid it on one side, and proceeded to lift out the boxes of explosive,

174

opening several of them for a quick check of the contents and separating one from the rest. He had replaced the automatic in a shoulder holster under his shirt and was now vulnerable if only Rafael could have extricated himself from under his number board silently and in one jump. Antón had moved. Rafael could only see that he had left the wellhead and become — probably — that shapeless blotch near the edge of the drilling platform which did not seem to have been there before. He was just too far away for a noiseless attack while the man's back was turned. Either by sheer telepathy or his alert, decisive movements this professional from the outside world gave the impression that he could pull his gun in a second and that no charge had a hope of succeeding.

As he bent to take out another box, Antón crouched with toes on the edge of the platform and launched himself through the air onto his back. Even so the shock was not conclusive, for both were lightly built. As Rafael, slower and more clumsy, stumbled out from hiding, a bullet kicked up the gravel at his feet. Though Antón was clamped to his enemy, pinioning his arms, the man had still managed to draw his gun, apparently firing between his knees as the pair rolled over. It was still far from all over when Rafael had fastened on his wrist and disarmed him. Short of killing him there was nothing for it but to jam him down on his face and lie spread-eagled over the writhing body until the rest of the party came up to add their weight.

They lifted him to his feet with his hands tied behind his back and a belt tight round his ankles. Rafael, touching the trigger of the splendid pistol, loosed off a shot which narrowly missed a box of gelignite.

"I should put on the safety catch if I were you," the stranger said.

He held himself upright and, so far as was possible, carelessly. There was a set smile on half his mouth in spite of blood which trickled from it through the paste of oil and sand.

"Your name?"

"On a job of this sort I am known as El Vicario."

"Well, Vicar, who sent you?"

"Man, if I am paid I do not ask questions."

"You hid these explosives when you came here the first time."

"Since you know so much, yes."

"And tonight you were going to use them."

"You're wrong there, mate. I was going to take them away."

"You lie! Do you want me to kill you?"

"No. But it seems likely you will anyway."

"Search him!"

Antón went through his pockets, at the same time giving him a vicious prick with his knife, and pulled out a roll of notes.

"He hasn't the sense to leave his money at home," Antón said.

"This? This I got here."

"From whom?"

"From your police captain. Since he is not my employer, I have no objection to telling you."

"Then it was the Government which sent you!" Rafael exclaimed.

"Those pickpockets? It was not! This money was a sweetener. A little tip such as sometimes comes one's way."

"Who gave it to Gonzalez?"

"I can tell you that. The Company."

"The Company knew about *Rosita?*"

"It would seem so, since I was expected."

"Ask him whether he killed Lorenzo, Chief!" said one of Rafael's men.

Rafael did not reply, but El Vicario had no hesitation.

"If you mean this fellow in the boots whom I dug up, I did not kill him. He keeps remarkably well in this climate, but you can see for yourselves that he was killed neither today nor two months ago. Also he died from a knife in the throat which is not my practice though you cannot be supposed to know it."

"Did the Company find out where this stuff was?" Rafael asked.

"It seems they did not, or why should they want me to collect it instead of digging it up themselves?"

The money in his pocket was strong evidence that his story was true; he really had been employed to remove the explosives from Cabo Desierto. Rafael, already feeling guilty in the presence of the crumpled Lorenzo and impressed in spite of himself by the courage of the living, could not make up his mind.

"Look! I have no objection to leaving you this little lot," El Vicario said. "But I can see you do not want it known that you have it."

"That's how it is," Rafael answered more peaceably. "So I cannot let you return to your boat empty-handed."

"I have heard there are other ways back to the Capital. There was, I believe, some trouble with your women."

"You will die!" Antón screamed.

"If I must. But do not forget I belong to your class, mates, and have fought for it!"

"Fought for it? Scab! Assassin! You were paid to cut off our water and break the boycott."

"I tell you this, friend. I have never taken money from the State or the Capitalists."

"It was our Union then?" Rafael asked.

"As you wish."

So the Union it was and Don Mateo's hint was right. Who could have believed it? By God, it was all beyond a plain carpenter trying to fight decently! First Antón and needless killing, then the betrayal of Gil Delgado and now this infamy of the Union.

"Didn't you understand that you would starve us out?"

"I do not read the papers. They make me sick. Oil, railways, companies, banks — we do not need them. Pay me for my trouble, and boom goes a piece of their property."

"You are right," Rafael said, for the man's passion to destroy what existed fitted his own mood of disgust. "We do not need them. But the innocent must not suffer."

"Then may I remind you that I am one?"

Not so innocent as he pretended. If the money was good, he didn't want to ask questions. But El Vicario knew how a man ought to die. And that was something, more than something. Rafael could not have told exactly what it was which appealed to him across the centuries, but it was there.

It was impossible to let him return to the boat. The fake

fishing captain was in this up to the neck; so were Gonzalez and Don Mateo. El Vicario would have to tell them that the militant workers had the explosives and might also mention Lorenzo. His throat ought to be cut then and there. What else could be done with him? Perhaps he might be allowed later on to attempt the land journey or to steal a boat and try his luck on the open sea. As likely as not he would cross a frontier and keep clear of those crooks at the Union.

But mercy was troublesome. It needed planning. And El Vicario was not an easy customer; he'd escape if he could. The company houses were not built to hold prisoners of — at a guess — considerable experience, and a permanent guard could not be posted without neighbors showing curiosity. Now that the field was split, nothing could be kept secret from Gil Delgado and his party.

His mind ran over deep holes in the ground and tanks — places with unclimbable walls where El Vicario could be held as long as necessary. But there were no wells in Cabo Desierto, and anyone dropped into a tank would be fried in his fat by sunset. In the refinery there must be cool tanks, if any of them were clean. The refinery, however, was a mystery like the Sentinels, to be guarded but not touched: a coiling cooker with wisps of vapor and pipes of flame where only the technicians could know what tank would kill — probably all of them whether empty or not.

The thought of metal in the sun brought to mind the shining tops of the distant tank farm and the afternoon — so long ago it seemed — with Uriarte. Uriarte was a possible ally. He had concrete silos, well shaded, well washed out when all the grass had been fed to the dairy herd. It was worth a try. No one except his own guards at the Charca would be on the road to the farm. If Uriarte could not be convinced — well then, there was nothing for it but Antón and his knife.

Rafael put back the few boxes which had been taken out, laid Lorenzo on top of them and replaced the cover. He ordered El Vicario's legs to be untied and marched him down to the truck. One of his men who could drive well enough for a straightforward journey took the wheel while he and Antón lay down in the back with their prisoner. The first crossroads and the hairpin bends down to the plain were empty. At the lower junction, close to the town, where the road to the farm branched off, the truck must have been seen, but there was no reason why it should attract any attention.

They stopped short of the Farm Manager's house and Rafael went on alone. Uriarte, warned by the approaching headlights, was waiting for him inside the gate.

"Well, and did you find your saboteur?" he asked skeptically.

"I have him here."

"And his explosives?"

"He has not told me where they are."

Perfectly true. Rafael had learned the trick of feminine prevarication during the years of peace and laughter with Catalina. She claimed fiercely that she never told a lie.

"You are sure you have the right man?"

"He has confessed that he was sent by the Union to destroy the Charca."

"And still alive?"

"I will not let them kill him in cold blood, Don Manuel. That is my difficulty. But I cannot let him go."

"Why not tell Don Mateo?"

"Impossible! He knew of this. It was he who told me to set a guard on the Charca. Me, his enemy! If he could have prevented the disaster any other way, he would have done so."

It was the first time that such a thought had occurred to Rafael and, now that it had, he took it as true. His need and his own eloquence suppressed, for himself as well as Uriarte, the fact that El Vicario was taking the explosives away.

"I cannot help you, Rafael. I am as angry as you, but I am a servant of the Company."

"If I cannot find a safe place for him I must kill him."

"There is no safe place here."

"Yes. An empty silo. He cannot climb out. And I can feed him and talk to him. You need know nothing."

"But if he calls for help someone will hear him."

"There is no place where your men do not come?"

"Of course there isn't. Do you give me your word that in the end you will let him go?"

"Yes, I swear. I will send him out secretly by land with food and water and a guide for the first part of the track. After that he must take his chance."

"Well, that's more than he deserves. A silo won't do, Rafael, but I have a cellar under the shed where I keep my seedlings. What sort of man is he?"

"A kind of anarchist, but valiant and well spoken."

"Not a man to break all my pots in a rage?"

"He has destroyed so much, I think, that he would not

break things meanly for fun. He will stay there calmly, planning how to escape."

"Then come and see my dungeon and tell me if it will do."

It had been a cistern in the early days of the farm. Uriarte had built over it a laboratory-cum-potting-shed for his own private hobby: the introduction from more temperate zones of flowering shrubs able to flourish under the partial shade of eucalyptus or in the patios of the town. A light, steel ladder led down from the shed to the cistern, which had a cool, even temperature and adjustable ventilation. The walls of smooth concrete were ten feet high.

"Pull up the ladder, and he can't climb out of there!" Uriarte said.

"I'll go and fetch him. Don't be alarmed at his appearance, Don Manuel! It is nothing but blood and oil, and he shall be washed before we put him down."

El Vicario, who had been ruthlessly suppressed in the bottom of the truck, seemed puzzled by the civilized comfort of the house to which he had been taken and was most deferential to the good fellow who fussed over him with the farm's first aid box. At the same time his eyes searched doors and windows. Rafael observed that he had slipped one hand free from its binding though still holding them both together.

"You told me this was the safety catch," he remarked, pushing it forward with a click.

Uriarte led the three into his potting shed, opened the trapdoor over the cistern, and went down the ladder with a rubber mattress, bread, cheese, water and a bottle of wine.

"Most kind!" El Vicario said, looking down into his

prison. "But permit me to remind you that I shall have no corkscrew."

Uriarte apologized for his thoughtlessness and added more sternly:

"I only do this to save your life. May I ask you to respect my plants?"

"If, as I suspect, you won't trust yourself down there alone with me and if you will lower a can with your instructions I will not only respect them but water them for you."

"Enough words!" Antón exclaimed. "Down, son of a whore, and may you rot there!"

Uriarte undid the prisoner's hands and feet. Covered by his own automatic and the Mayor's formidable revolver, El Vicario shrugged his shoulders and went down the ladder. Rafael pulled it up behind him, slammed the trapdoor into place and quickly fixed a bolt to it.

"Thank you a thousand times, Don Manuel," he said. "I shall come tomorrow. But now we must hurry to return the truck."

The party drove back without lights, for starshine on the straight road past the communal lands was enough. Rafael told the driver to stop short of the town, intending to leave the truck there, but Antón could never resist a chance to show contempt.

"El Vicario told us where the truck was left for him. There is no better place and we will put it back there. We have only to pass behind the Town Hall and then down the backs of the shops towards the port. Never a policeman there! And Gonzalez himself will be watching the quay."

"As you wish," Rafael answered, weary of command. "I shall get out here and go home. Until tomorrow!"

He was overcome by tiredness and careless with El Vicario's pistol. He flung it down with his clothes at the foot of the couch in the living room which had become his bed. The bedroom where he had slept with Catalina had been handed over to Chepe. He felt that the memories which to him were intolerable might mean to Chepe a continuing security, the next best thing to Catalina herself.

The boy was sound asleep, clutching against his cheek his very private object, small, shapeless and black with dirt. It had been an absorbent pad taken from his mother's drawer, but was now hardly recognizable. Chepe had tied a string round one end so that it could be imagined to have a head and body. Rafael, when he first noticed it and realized what it was, wanted to throw it away. That was the only time he had ever reduced Chepe to hysterical resistance.

He overslept heavily. Chepe was already up, tiptoeing about. Forbidden to use the stove, he had laid out the fruit and bread for breakfast and picked up his father's clothes as Catalina used to do. When Rafael at last opened his eyes, Chepe had the automatic in his hands, fascinated by such sleek, smooth blackness with all sorts of little purposeful protuberances. Rafael snatched it away from him, thankful for that not too obvious safety catch.

"Where did you get it, papacito?"

"From a friend whom you do not know."

"It is for killing people if they are no use?"

"It is for killing people, but, man . . ."

"Like Gil Delgado?"

"No, not like Gil Delgado."

"Like Captain Gonzalez?" Chepe persisted.

"It is true that he is no use. But one must remember he has children."

"If he didn't have children, would you kill him?"

"Not if he leaves us in peace."

"Don Mateo has no children."

"Don Mateo has nothing!" Rafael replied in a sudden burst of resentment. "And he is nothing. Nothing but eyes!"

"But if you killed him, he would be dead like our mother."

"Of course he'd be dead," Rafael answered impatiently.

Chepe was silent and got on with his breakfast. He knew very well that if you killed people they were dead; but, as it were, in theory only. His mother was dead, and the Company had killed her; that was an article of faith. He was going to kill Gonzalez when he was big enough; that was another article of faith. But then there would be no Gonzalez, never any more Gonzalez. He was overcome by the shock of reality, that second birth at seven years old as startling as the first. The dream of killing revealed itself as the grim fact of death. Don Mateo had become part of his universe. Yet to his father Don Mateo was no use, and nothing could be done about it.

Rafael plodded along the road to the Company Farm, quite unaware that Catalina's hummingbird had suffered a change as irreversible as if the safety catch had been off, and was regarding its fallen wings in a passion of tears inexplicable to itself. He regretted his flash of invective against the General Manager — not that Chepe, accustomed to be talked to as if he were an equal companion, would take an early-morning mood seriously, but Don Mateo was a grave and gigantic friend.

He understood to perfection this affair going on under his nose, and was very proud that his son was irresistible. He and Catalina used to dream of the quick, honorable man he might become and how far he would go beyond a simple carpenter in an oil field. And then the gentleness of Don Mateo, which exasperated him because he had no very clear answer to it, had a humorous geniality when directed to his son. All his companions appreciated the irony and innocence of it, though Rafael had never mentioned the incident which started it off.

He found Manuel Uriarte busy weighing piglets and disinclined for conversation. Evidently he regretted that he had been bounced into acting as an amateur jailer and was anxious to disassociate himself from the whole unsavory business. At last he took Rafael to one side and gave him the key of the potting shed, telling him to lock it behind him and keep his voice low. He would come along later, he said, and supply whatever was wanted for the prisoner's comfort.

Rafael opened the trapdoor and found El Vicario entertaining himself by making a chessboard with little piles of lime and soot.

"Breakfast will be coming. Is there anything else you need?"

"Something to piss in, mate. I have done my best to be decent but all the flowerpots have holes in the bottom. And I must remind you that I have one, too."

"The devil! We are not experienced, and with all that excitement . . ."

He searched the shed and lowered a bucket and some newspaper on the end of a string.

"Many thanks! And now, if it is no secret, tell me where I am."

"At the Company Farm which you wished to destroy."

"I? What makes you think that? For me, all of us should live on the land or at a craft."

The man had something about him of a salesman at a fair — gallantly self-confident, but one doubted if he could be telling the truth. Rafael explained shortly and contemptuously what effect the destruction of the Charca would have on the boycott.

"And so this Charca is not the main water supply after all?"

"Of course not! Our water comes from high in the mountains."

"Your Union said not a word of that or of farms. They told me that without its water the Company must surrender."

"It's true you do not ask questions! And when they paid you to return and take away the explosives, what did they say then?"

"Nothing. I supposed the Company had made it worth their while. Those dirty little caciques will always change their minds for money. Why are they against you?"

"They are socialists. They said the State was right. So we threw them in the harbor. Here we are in Cabo Desierto, not Russia!"

"Are the Sentinels guarded by the police or the Company?"

"Neither. I hold them."

"Then why are they still there, mate?"

"It is impossible — even if one were to cut off the Christmas Tree with a blowtorch."

"For a professional, nothing is impossible. When your men get tired of keeping me alive, remember that!"

"My men will do what I tell them."

"Sometimes before you tell them. Another inch and your friend's knife would have been in my liver."

"And why not? A little lesson for your employers!"

Rafael dropped the hatch. He sat down outside the shed waiting for Uriarte and cursing this irrepressible Spaniard who forced on him a brutality which was not in his character. Besides that, it was going to be most difficult to feed him with servants about in the kitchen and the house. For the time being Uriarte settled that problem by ordering a large breakfast for Rafael and himself carrying it off to the potting shed. The only satisfaction in the whole awkward business was the ingenious sling which Rafael knotted for lowering the tray intact, coffee and all. Mercy was proving too dangerous. It might possibly be repaid at the cost of letting the devil loose; but the effect of that was as incalculable as keeping him where he was.

ELEVEN. The morning brought no news of El Vicario. He had vanished over some horizon of his own as completely as *Rosita* into the Pacific. Gonzalez found some blood on the floor of the truck — not enough, he thought, for any serious wound, but without laboratory analysis of the oily dirt it was impossible to be sure. The temperature of the field, which Mat had tried so hard to keep under control, was — well, one couldn't say that it

189

was rising, but there were too many unknowns in the furnace. Birenfield, with echoes of Dave Gunner's ponderous whispers in his ears, was already responsible for two probable murders and the presence of a hundred and fifty kilos of gelignite which, please God, nobody had found or would find. Yet there was no proof at all of his complicity. As for Garay, if he didn't kill Lorenzo, it was a hundred to one that he knew who did and why. He might already be feeling the cornered animal against which Luis Solano had given his warning.

As Mat strolled back to his house for lunch he was aware of Chepe dodging in and out of the palms and shrubs behind him. He could not be sure whether the boy wanted to talk or whether he was merely — poor little blighter! — observing his hero at a distance. He decided to walk on and leave it to the boy to do fearlessly whatever he had come up the hill to do.

On the bare bit of road between the executive ghetto and his house Chepe was still following and could no longer pretend he wasn't; so Mat turned and walked back to him. The boy had none of his usual confidence. He only murmured a reply to cheerful greetings and immediately pulled a small and filthy lump from inside his shirt, thrusting it into Mat's hands. His eyes were on the ground — an entirely new and bashful Chepe — except for a second when he lifted them to Mat's face with what was plainly an appeal. Then, again unlike any known Chepe, he ran.

The whole act was untranslatable. If Mat had been dealing with an adult who looked at him with the same expression and the same slight air of guilt, he would have assumed the man was desperately trying to say "keep this safe for me," as if the police were after him and his only chance was to hand over to a stranger. But who the devil was going to take it, whatever it was, away from Chepe, and why should he want to get rid of it?

The thought intruded, instantly to be dismissed, that the object might blow up. Mat pinched it. There was nothing inside. If it had a couple of legs sewn on, it would look like a doll. He played with the idea that in fact it was a doll, that he was expected to provide legs and that Chepe was too embarrassed at possessing such a plaything to say what he wanted. That, however, must be fantasy. While he might be a sort of extra father able to mend a mechanical toy, he couldn't possibly be a mother who sewed legs on dolls. He put the thing in his pocket and carried it home, carefully concealing it in a collar box from Pepe and Amelia. That was the least he could do. The secret could not be explained but evidently it was a very intimate one belonging to both himself and Chepe.

Returning to the office he found a message from the Mayor that the last of the seriously injured policemen was being discharged from hospital and would leave for the Capital on the evening launch; he himself would be at the quay to wish him well on behalf of the community and he wondered if Don Mateo would also like to be present. Mat saw no reason why he should. A letter of thanks on behalf of the Company and a generous check was the usual procedure. To turn up on the quay could appear a trifle provocative at a time when his every action was read as meaning something or other which it didn't. He asked Pilar what she thought and received the haughty reply that he was above all such nonsense and might as well go and find out what the Mayor really wanted.

There was no delegation on the quay — just the Mayor, Captain Gonzalez and Jane Thorpe as chairwoman of the hospital committee. The Mayor did not appear to want anything or, if he did, was even vaguer than usual. After a string of compliments he strolled off with Gonzalez, and Mat invited Mrs. Thorpe to join him in something long and cold under the colonnade. He admired her for herself and her three languages — excellent Spanish, a formal standard English which she kept for Mrs. Gateson and the country club and a marked west-country accent which she used at home with her husband and intimate friends.

"I cannot imagine why His Worship wanted me," he said. "Am I the only reliable witness to his whereabouts at six in the evening?"

Jane Thorpe laughed.

"I told him I wanted to talk to you," she replied.

A clever woman! She knew very well that he was inclined to resent feminine influence, but that he would only be amused if she admitted it at once. It wasn't surprising that the Mayor had obeyed her. No doubt Jane was busy patching up his matrimonial differences.

"And telephoned Pilar to make sure I came?"

"Of course!"

"What's so private and urgent, Jane?"

"Chepe. When Ray had left for the office, I found the child hanging round the house waiting."

"Any hint of peace?"

"No, worse news. He couldn't come to you directly with it."

"Jane, I have never used him in that way," Mat said, quick to deny the implication that he cultivated Chepe as a useful informer. "I think his father knows it, though of course he wouldn't tell Chepe more than he must. The boy's integrity — that's what matters! You'll understand. You're the only person who could. What's bothering him?"

"He believes Rafael means to kill you."

"Nonsense! You know that as well as I do."

"Well, yes," she answered doubtfully. "But Rafael has changed."

"Whatever put it into the child's head?"

"He wouldn't say. Loyalty. Just what you were talking about. And he was quite incoherent. Something about you being no use."

"I saw him this morning."

He told Jane Thorpe of the inexplicable incident and the doll-like lump which he had taken home.

"Yes, I've seen it."

"What is it?"

"Something that belonged to Catalina."

"But why give it to me?"

"I think I see, but I'm not sure. Mat, did you ever have a teddy bear or anything when you were young?"

"I suppose so, but I've forgotten."

"Well, if you've forgotten you won't understand. But to Chepe it means security, protection, love, everything."

"But then he wouldn't give it away."

"Protection, Mat. Think about that!"

"You mean, his personal little god to look after me?"

"If we could put that into seven-year-old language. Ask Luis Solano!"

"I'm damned if I do."

"Oh, what a lot of privacies you have! You see why I had to talk to you alone."

"Ray . . . well . . ."

"He'd understand the teddy bear angle much better than you," she retorted. "Anyway, I didn't know about that. What I was afraid of was that Ray would take any threat to your life far too seriously. He'd do anything for you and he's impulsive."

"Fearless too, bless him! But I'm as sure of Garay as of myself. He must often have shouted that he'd like to bump me off. And if it comes to that I've been asked before now if I would approve an accident being arranged for him. Probably he let himself go and the child misunderstood him."

"But you'll be careful, Mat, won't you?"

"Within reason. What's going on at the port?"

The evening seemed noisier than usual though nothing very definite could be distinguished since the excitement was round the corner at the bottom of the main street. The launch might have narrowly missed an incoming boat or a lorry might have backed into a pile of crates or the police, most improbably, might have hauled an incapable drunk into the station. In such cases the lookers-on took sides eagerly and went on expressing their opinions until they were hoarse or bored, or the original contestants had slunk off to settle the argument in peace, alarmed at the enthusiasm of their backers.

A small crowd emerged into the main street, not coming forward as in a demonstration but moving slowly backwards with their eyes on the attraction. This center of gravity as in turn it surged round the corner seemed to be moving sideways — the effect of two parties on each side of the road continually turning to face each other. Marching up the middle were Rafael Garay and Gil Delgado stopping at intervals to exchange remarks, their extremes of color very marked among the browns of the surrounding faces.

"Better get inside, Jane," Mat said.

"Where are the police?"

"In the station, where they should be."

No, one didn't want the police. He remembered telling Dave Gunner that they used to give them the day off to go fishing, and it was true. But the Company then had the daring and geniality of youth. Now there wasn't any Company except himself. He continued to sit at his table almost alone. The rest of the outside customers had discreetly disappeared or had joined the backward-moving crowd, curiosity overcoming the risk of being caught in an eruption of violence.

As the fuming couple came abreast of the café, Rafael turned on his General Manager, partly provoked by his casual, cross-legged loneliness, partly invited by a confident wave of the hand.

"Hola, you! This arse-licker of yours says there are no funds to pay us."

"Where are you going?"

"To the bank!"

"But it is shut."

"Then it will be opened."

The band of Rafael's followers on the near side of the road turned away from their opponents to watch the unexpected conversation. There were only a dozen of them, but those the toughest of the oil workers, well able to hold their own in any set-to with the larger crowd behind Delgado.

"A lot of good you will get from the bank! The manager will be hiding under the counter. He is not one of us."

One of us. That note again which always bewildered Rafael. Don Mateo must feel it. Clever devil as he was, it could not be a pose.

"And you! What do you know about this?"

"Nothing, friend. I am not a cashier."

"Leave him alone, Rafael!" Delgado yelled. "This is not for him or the Company."

"At least he is honest."

"Tell me I lie again and we come to blows!"

"I think I had better fetch a policeman," Mat said.

There was an instant's silence at so senseless a remark, and then it burst on the two factions. What a type, this Don Mateo!

He took the opportunity to stride out and join the leaders, his glass still in his hand.

"Friends, this can be settled without blowing up the bank. One of you says that it has no funds, the other that it has. You are not the only ones to suffer from banks and their rules and their papers. It is perfectly possible that you are both right. If you will come to my office tomorrow, Don Rafael, I will have the facts for you."

"I do not visit your office like this Judas!"

"As you wish. Then where?"

"Where our women are buried!" Rafael retorted, carried away by his anger and not meaning a literal appointment.

"That is a promise?"

"If you come alone."

"I shall come alone this evening."

Rafael gathered up his men with a sweep of the arm and led them away, pushing contemptuously through Delgado's supporters. He had never intended this confrontation which had started behind the port offices where the new boycott committee was distributing relief funds to the needy. The amount available had been dying away for some time as the professionally benevolent became bored with Cabo Desierto and the oil workers of the continent lost interest in supporting a boycott which had been publicized as unreasonable and against the advice of the Union. There had, however, been one anonymous and substantial transfer from Zurich every week. Gil Delgado announced to the meeting that the bank told him it had not arrived and that future payments had been cancelled.

Normally Rafael would have accepted the fact since none of those in most need was among his supporters, but his nerves were ragged after two days of holding and feeding El Vicario without any practical plan for getting rid of him. He burst out that his people were being victimized and accused Delgado of trying to bring them to heel by starvation. Gil had no trouble in refuting the accusation. Rafael's men, he said, were among the most competent of the peasants. That in itself was offensive, for it suggested that they kept part of the communal produce for themselves. But there was a more brutal bit of his vulgarity to come. Many, he added, were without families and had only themselves to keep. It was a marvel that men who had lost their wives did not storm the committee then and there.

As committee and protesters turned into the main street Rafael was near to losing control of his men and himself and knew it. The unexpected presence of the General Manager was a relief. He could be used as a distraction. That was the main motive behind his deliberately rude response.

Well, he would have to meet him now; and nobody after that public exchange could accuse him of slinking round to the office to talk in private. He felt confident of holding his own better in the dark, and of dominating mere eyes by his physical superiority.

Antón insisted that he should post a few reliable men up among the sand hills and go armed. He agreed. That Don Mateo would try to assassinate him or have him kidnapped was unthinkable, but there were others in the Company — that Gateson for one — and how far they might go was uncertain. They distrusted their General Manager. One could see it in the matter of the Charca. Why was he unable to guard the water himself?

The little cemetery was a lonely spot out beyond the refinery and not far from the shacks where those guiltless, terrified women had picked up their children and escaped. The Cabo Desierto cemetery was full, so the priest had consecrated new ground. A lot of nonsense! What would happen to those dead was neither better nor worse than to Catalina, a pulp hurled up and down between the fury of the surf and the green peace of deep water until it was eaten by the crabs.

The ground was surrounded by a low wall, hastily built. He came early and sat there waiting. The sea itself gave some light so that the wall was white and monotonous as the breakers. Don Mateo was visible a hundred yards away as he walked along the beach — a moving rod, tall and black, against the milkiness of the spent terraces of the surf.

"So you have come, Don Rafael!"

"And why not?"

"Several reasons, friend, for you as for me."

"I have nothing against you personally, Don Mateo. Chepe — I have not forgotten."

"It is nothing. The child deserves all we can give."

"He has too much freedom, but you will understand my time is not my own."

Rafael felt no more of his intended domination. He was only conscious of equality in loneliness. Don Mateo for the moment had become the vague patriarchal adviser for whom he had so often felt a need. That would not do. He was there to listen to him about banks.

"Have you anything to say or not?" he asked aggressively. "What do you know of this swindle of Delgado's?"

"A lot. Delgado told the truth. It's a dirty business, but you had better know where your weekly subvention came from."

"Do not tell me from Russia, for I shall not believe it."

"You would be right. It came from an oil company — one of the biggest which hopes to buy Cabo Desierto cheap."

"How did you find out?"

"Because I myself was suspected of taking this money to keep the boycott alive."

"You? There are people without shame or decency."

It was Henry Constantinides in far-off London who had supplied the information. There in London Wall Henry

must have envisaged his General Manager smoothly in-
sinuating the facts — if necessary at all — into the ear of
some urbane visitor from Embassy or Government, not
frankly exposing them to his enemy, both together among
the rusty cans and refuse on the edge of an eternity.

It had been obvious that Gateson's accusation could not
be a mere shot in the dark; the Field Manager, however
angry, was not fool enough for that. There had to be some
basis of fact: perhaps a private letter from Birenfield or
some former colleague repeating a rumor which was running through the underground of the oil industry. Mat had
at once cabled to Henry, whose discreet inquiries through
the head office of the Cabo Desierto bank, aided by his
interlocking directorships, revealed the identity of the generous benefactor; but attempts to prove it came up against
a dead end — so dead that it stank to high heaven. Why
the weekly payments had stopped was anybody's guess,
possibly because the boycott — to any outside observer —
now seemed certain to collapse or because the donors had
been warned of Henry's investigation.

Mat explained to Rafael as simply as he could the
motives of his charitable sympathizers.

"So we were paid just to change one oil company for
another?"

"These things happen, friend. Don't blame yourself!"

Still another illusion gone. Even if he had known he
would probably have accepted the money and laughed at
the crooks who sent it — with the help of Gil Delgado's
cynicism. Though he didn't blame himself, he felt a need to
excuse himself. He stumbled over words to explain the
contradiction.

"Don Mateo, suppose you told me to make a rotten locker for the launch. I would not refuse, but I would make a good one. That is the only way I can work."

"Of course. You are a man of honor."

"It is a shame that you were not here when the old field was closed down."

"Thank you. But I am here now. Tell me frankly — what have you to gain? I have got for you what you wanted."

"No! Without oil, yes."

"But the Sentinels exist."

"And our women and children? Those that rot here?"

"As you said, there are people without decencies. That is why there is such a thing as forgiveness."

"There is too much in this world, Mr. Manager. If it is to move there must be an end to forgiveness."

"Doña Catalina would not have agreed with you."

"That may be, but she was a saint."

"I have heard it said that there is something of that in you, too — wrong way up."

"Who said that?"

"Believe me or not — Gonzalez."

"Gonzalez learned his lesson. So there has been no more violence."

"Lorenzo?"

"I do not want to know anything of Lorenzo."

"But you can't help it, Don Rafael. And there will be more Lorenzos if you and I cannot understand each other."

"I will never sit down with Gil Delgado."

"It isn't necessary if you will sit down with me. Delgado wants to remain an oil worker. You and yours do not. All we have to discuss is the land and the water and more capital if you need it — a committee of the Mayor, Thorpe, ourselves and Uriarte perhaps and anyone else you choose."

The mention of Uriarte broke the spell. Rafael shied away from all prospect of negotiation. Nothing could be done until he had got rid of El Vicario and his hands were clean.

"Don Mateo, this is my duty, and, believe me, I have no pleasure in it."

"But you will meet me again?"

"Of course. You came alone as you said."

"So did you."

A tactful reply. Mat kept to himself the fact that he had spotted a match lighting two cigarettes among the sand hills. Anyway, he had been sure of Garay, though doubtful how far the man could ensure the obedience of his followers.

"I? That means nothing!" Rafael answered angrily.

That extraordinary husband of Catalina! The tactful reply had been a bad mistake. Garay had been made to feel the lesser man. He was always at the mercy of genuine conscience. It was not the kind of inferiority complex which one could foresee and reckon with.

"Meanwhile, a bit of advice! Keep your guards on the Charca!"

Rafael was surprised and out of his depth. That seemingly simple remark needed someone like Gil to translate it. Don Mateo knew of the landing of El Vicario and must know that he had not left. What else did he know? Perhaps it was a trap or perhaps he was afraid that El Vicario was at large with the explosives.

"Why not you?" Rafael retorted. "Put some of your clerks up there! They can look at their collars and ties in the water."

"It's obvious why not. Your men would suspect that I was holding the Charca in order to destroy it."

"But now we know it is not your policy."

Mat realized that he should never have mentioned the Charca. Another mistake! He had hoped to find out from Rafael's reply whether El Vicario was safely dead or not. Such sparring for position was stupid when the bond of sympathy existed and was half-admitted. He took refuge in honesty.

"Look! We both know there are secrets we cannot yet tell and we both know what about. Leave it so — but it's the devil that neither of us can trust the only man who counts."

"You feel that, too? But you are the General Manager."

"What does that matter? And you are a good carpenter. We do what we think we must and it is never enough to win."

"That may be true, Don Mateo, for there are times when I do not see how either of us can lose."

Rafael walked back with him as far as the town to keep his men from showing themselves prematurely. He felt more peace in himself. If he called off the boycott — he allowed himself the "if" without admitting any intention — it would not be surrender to the Company but an agreement with Don Mateo. Both avoided the subject, talking a little of neutrals whom they liked, such as the

Mayor and Dr. Solano, and then of Chepe's future — a
difficult subject for Mat since any mention of grants and
apprenticeships implied the continued existence of the
Company. He was content to say cautiously that wherever
he might be he was always ready to be consulted.

At the tank farm Rafael stopped and held out his hand.
He would have liked to go on talking and perhaps have a
drink with his enemy, but he could not be seen in the street
on such friendly terms. Don Mateo appeared to appreciate
that, and went on by himself into the lights of the quayside
where he had left his car. He was slightly bent with weariness and no longer the bold figure which had come out of
the night. Rafael could not have said what it was he
wanted for him — at any rate some more human form of
relaxation than the society of all those crooks up the hill.

Antón and his men joined their leader, all asking at once
what the Manager had to say of Gil Delgado's swindle.
Their curiosity seemed irrelevant. For Rafael, the original
object of the dialogue had slipped away into unimportance.

"That? A bribe! We are better without it. A thing of
other oil companies, friends, who are as dirty as the Union."

He walked on to his house, expecting to find Chepe in
bed, but the boy was still up and waiting for him. He
seemed to have eaten very little. His large eyes were darker
than usual and his neck seemed too childishly fragile to
hold up his head.

"Where have you been, papacito?"

"Talking to your friend, Don Mateo."

"And what happened?"

"Nothing. Why?"

"Nothing at all? You promise?"

"I promise. You have no need to be afraid, Chepe. I would trust myself with Don Mateo anywhere. You know what a true man he is."

"What did you talk about?"

"About you, little one, sometimes."

"What did he tell you?"

"Such a lot of questions! For one thing he told me that you will be a man to be proud of."

"Will he always be in Cabo Desierto?"

"I hope so, Chepe."

Rafael caught himself up sharply. He didn't hope so. One could hardly imagine Don Mateo renting a bit of land from the community and settling down.

"That is something we will see," he added at once. "And if he is not here I can send you to London with a little note saying 'This is Chepe.' "

"But he would know it was Chepe."

"No, he wouldn't — not when you are taller than your father with smart shoes!"

The child laughed and laughed. Rafael did not think his remark all that funny, but he was aware that some sort of cloud had blown over. Chepe was obsessed with killing. That was his own fault. Yet surely he could never have believed his father in danger from his other hero, Don Mateo? When he went into the bedroom to see if his son was asleep and to adore him like a silent shepherd if he was, he noticed that the vile rag which he held against his cheek was missing. Well, if he had lost it, that accounted for his puzzling mood. He must remember to ask about it in the morning.

He did not remember, having El Vicario on his mind.

The man was no use — a phrase Chepe had solemnly used some time or other — but he did not deserve a bullet in the back of the neck. The only other way out was to steal a boat and let him take his chance. El Vicario could not go far wrong if he was over the horizon before dawn and thereafter kept the coast in sight. And what he said to the lumps of dung who paid him mattered to nobody but himself.

When Rafael reached the Company Farm to attend to his prisoner's daily requirements, he found Uriarte deep in discussion with Thorpe. Uriarte was nervous, naturally enough, and not at all pleased to see him; but Thorpe at once dragged him into the conversation. That was like Sr. Thorpe — always expansive and impulsive and on tiptoe. One could never begin to dislike him.

"Now, here's a man who will want a bit of land of his own!" Thorpe said.

"No, Mr. Superintendent. When the Company is no more I shall work for the community."

"Rafael, I cannot understand why a man like you doesn't see sense. The Sentinels can't just disappear."

"But they will give no oil."

"You're crazy! You've won all along the line — frightened that bastard Birenfield off, chucked out your lousy Union and got a General Manager whom you all like!"

"What I think of Don Mateo has nothing to do with it."

"By God, it has! You know very well that he could give us all a happy field again with your own houses and the right to work on the land."

"He cannot give back our women and children whom the

Company killed. I have much respect for you, Mr. Superintendent, but it is you who will not understand."

"Listen! If it's just the women, it's about time you knew
the truth."

"What truth? We have enough of excuses and apologies.
The Company refused to let their husbands back and they
were all alone and terrified of the police."

"I wish to Jesus they had been!"

"More lies from Birenfield and the Union?"

"Not from them, friend Rafael. From your Catalina and
my wife."

"I am listening."

Rafael heard the story in a turmoil of emotion. The
Company not to blame? But it doubled the blame and
smeared filth over the lot!

"Did you know this, Don Manuel?"

"Not I, Rafael! Nobody knows it."

"And you believe it?"

"Man, from anyone else I wouldn't. But neither of the
Thorpes would invent what Catalina said."

Yes, that was true. Though there was no echo at all of
Catalina in Thorpe's words, this must be what she had
heard from the women. Rafael asked whether Gonzalez
knew.

"Of course not! No idea of discipline! He never knows a
thing about his men and is full of information about everyone else."

"And Don Mateo?"

"I told him long ago. Now do you see? Your poor
martyrs were a lot of dirty whores!"

There was no end to disillusion. The murder of Lorenzo,

Gil Delgado, the money and now this. Don Mateo had been right to say nothing. He at least saw that this sordid story made no difference to the reason for the boycott and that the only effect would be to send widowers like Antón running wild with knives among guilty and innocent. The police deserved it. They might still get it. That depended on whether bloodshed could bring about the defeat of Delgado and the Company or not. But nothing mattered except that the oil should never flow again. All that remained clean was his own determination that it should be never.

"Look, Rafael!" Thorpe said reasonably. "You are alone. You have no support beyond a bunch of toughs without a brain in their heads. Even Chepe doesn't approve of you."

"Take care!"

"No dramatics, friend! It's nothing serious. Only some sort of doll he has which he gave to Don Mateo."

"Why?"

"God knows. My wife didn't tell me. Just affection, I suppose. Perhaps it was all he had to give."

"Then there is nothing left to me at all."

"Well, you may think that, but no one else does. How about that bit of land and a home you need never worry about and watching your strip of the corn grow while the rest of us are sweating it out for the shareholders?"

"Don Manuel, may I go to the house and see how my potted plant is doing?"

"Here is the key, Rafael. The Superintendent and I are going down to the edge of the beach where the water gate needs repair."

TWELVE. Rafael opened the trapdoor, savagely wishing that he had brought the automatic instead of leaving it on the rafters of his house, safely out of Chepe's reach. If there were anyone who was useless, it was El Vicario. But the man had advanced beyond the symmetry of a chessboard and laid out in lime and soot a silhouette of Cabo Desierto, at once recognizable from the exaggeration of the tank farm, the refinery and the Three

Sentinels. Such humanity disarmed the gun that wasn't there. He must have had long practice in cell art.

"Any time you want to get rid of me, mate," he said, "I would prefer some other death to starvation."

"You think this is a restaurant?"

"If it is, it's a long way from the kitchen."

Uriarte had concealed a fresh loaf and slices of meat in a locker. Rafael tossed them down to his prisoner and sat on the edge of the hatch silently watching him eat.

"You are not careful enough," El Vicario said with his mouth full. "One jump and I could catch your feet and pull you down."

"A lot of good that would do you!"

"One never knows. Something might present itself. I presume you would be missed. The trouble is: I don't know by whom."

"Nor do I."

"Depressed this morning, mate? I have observed that the usual cause is being deprived of all possibility of action."

"You are right. Everything would be simpler if I had you killed."

"Short and sharp never cures anything."

"It does not take long to dig a grave."

"But what a waste!"

"How a waste?"

"All that gelignite. Why not blow up the General Manager?"

"Give me something else to serve for him!"

"I believe I mentioned the Sentinels."

"And I told you it was impossible."

"When you watched me open up those boxes, did you see me put one by itself? That was my personal property, not the Union's."

"Your clothes? I saw a belt in it and some socks."

"Not clothes, mate. That is what we call a necklace, and I know of no neck it will not cut."

"There would be no more oil ever?"

"I should imagine not. Frankly I have no idea what would happen, but I should take care to be far away at the time."

"Far away? You can't! One match and pouf!"

"Friend Rafael — I believe that is your name? — things go off when I tell them to and not before."

"How do I know that you will not escape?"

"Two good reasons. One is that you will be holding my gun — yourself, please, not one of your more excitable assistants. The other is that I should enjoy the job. The crown, perhaps, of a career. But there is a difficulty."

"You have only to tell me."

"How can I know that you will not shoot me when all is ready for you?"

"You have my word."

"Well, you seem to be a man of honor, but appearances are deceptive. I tell you what. I will lay the charges and you can all of you watch me at work. However, I shall not teach you how to set them off safely until I am in a boat alone with the engine running."

"And if your stuff does not go up?"

"It will, mate, it will. And without risk to any of you. I tell you that as one craftsman to another. And then there will be one oil company the less."

"How long will it take?"

"My part of it? Half an hour for each well perhaps. But I must see the problem on the ground."

"If I can arrange everything I will come for you after dark."

Rafael shut him up, locked the door of the potting shed, and walked back to town. Problems which, when they were vague, had seemed perplexing, at once became simplified now that there was a definite objective. To lay hands on a boat and observe El Vicario's conditions were both easy. The lifeless refinery, unlit and picketed by his own men, had a small basin of its own within the breakwater where two boats were moored, out of sight of the port offices and the police barracks in the customs shed. El Vicario could safely be embarked. He might or might not be challenged as he ran for the harbor mouth, but by the time the harbormaster had been hauled out of bed — or, more probably, given orders from the window — El Vicario should be well away, close under the desert coast and unlikely to be caught or even spotted.

Rafael ate something and slept a little, with a worrying dream that he instead of El Vicario was alone on the ocean, only there was no boat, and sea and sky were of the same illimitable darkness. Then he wrote out in large capital letters a note for Chepe to find when he returned from school, telling him that he would be out all night and that there was nothing, nothing — a passionate NADA, NADA — to be afraid of.

He collected Antón and gave him his instructions. The guards on the Sentinels were to be reinforced, but casually, one by one, so that Delgado and his people would notice nothing. The refinery picket was to see that the better of the two boats had a full tank and plenty of food and water on board.

"Don't tell me that you are letting him go, Chief!"

"Yes. No one else can win for us."

"And how?"

"Not a word to anyone! Not even to think of it!"

"You can trust my mouth, Rafael, when I am not angry."

"He is going to blow up the Sentinels for us."

"Christ! There will be nothing left of Cabo Desierto. Three volcanoes!"

"Nonsense! We have all seen wells out of hand. This will be the same but a higher fountain. With luck the Sentinels will burn for months till there is no more oil in the ground."

"As you wish, Chief. But you won't catch me within a mile of them."

"El Vicario can arrange for them to go up while we are all eating our breakfast in peace. He has his secret methods."

"You have that much confidence in him?"

"I have none, Antón, and he will have a pistol at his back. But I think he will do what he promises. I shall take him up to 32 soon after nine. Have the boxes ready for us by the side of the hole."

"And Lorenzo?"

"Put him back afterwards. There is no better place. When you have done it, go across the golf course to 97 and bring the men back with you. We shall need them to carry the boxes."

At dusk Rafael went down to the refinery to check that the boat was ready and seaworthy. He then set out for the Company Farm, picking up on his way the two guards who had just come on duty at the Charca. He left them in the darkness outside the gate of Uriarte's house, went up the path and knocked at the door. Uriarte answered after some delay and quickly put his fingers to his lips to indicate that he was not alone in the curtained house.

"But I have come to take away your prisoner."

"Thank God for that! It's all right if you are quick."

He unlocked the potting shed for Rafael and helped him to lower the ladder. El Vicario came up without a word, giving a cheerful wink to Uriarte as if he were not covered all the way by his own gun in Rafael's hand. Outside the gate the Farm Manager saw two large shadows close in on his prisoner. It was a shock. In spite of the relentless boycott he had never connected his gentle and interested Rafael with firearms and what was surely going to be an execution.

As soon as they were clear of the farm, Rafael offered El Vicario a bottle.

"Thank you, but no! On these delicate operations I do not drink."

"We have two long walks ahead of us."

"In my time I have walked and run and crawled far enough to reach the moon, friend Rafael, and always there were the rifles of the police not far behind. See if you can keep up with me!"

He doubled the pace with a long, loping stride that was half a run. His body seemed to have no more weight than the cage of rusty wire which it resembled.

As a matter of pride the three accepted his pace along the flat. At the bottom of the rough path which cut across the hairpins of the road Rafael called enough, pointing out that there was a steep climb ahead and that it should be taken slowly and silently. At the top he waited to see if there were any lights moving on the road to the old field. It was deserted as usual. All activity was confined to the pools of shaded illumination in the executive quarter below and to their left, and the naked bulbs of the labor lines behind them.

At 32 they found Antón with the four men of the picket from 97. He had stacked the boxes at some distance from the abandoned well, and there was nothing to show where they had been. The planks were back in position with scrap and rubbish scattered over them.

"From now on I command under friend Rafael," El Vicario said, "who should keep me covered in order to inspire confidence in the rest of you. This box —" he picked up the one he had called his own — "holds the detonators and the tools of my trade. I shall carry it myself. Should you think it necessary to shoot, mate, be careful to hit some part of me and not the box."

The other ten boxes of fifteen kilos each were distributed among the party. Antón, with El Vicario at his side and Rafael immediately behind, led the way through the field, across the golf course and up to the Sentinels.

Inside the hut which housed 97, El Vicario examined the Christmas Tree with casual interest, remarking that a child could break it, that half a kilo would cut any pipe or valve they chose. Rafael, who had been told again and again by men of the drilling crews that no bomb or blowtorch would have any permanent effect on oil production, was disappointed. He had assumed that El Vicario appreciated exactly what he was up against.

"He knows nothing!" one of the skilled workers exclaimed contemptuously. "I will show him what he must cut — and God help us all if he can do it!"

He beckoned to a mate. The pair lifted the heavy flooring over the well cellar, revealing the base of the Christmas Tree and, below it, the massive valve clamped to the well head. Between the two flanges of base and valve was a steel gate five feet in circumference shaped like a neck and not much longer. El Vicario stroked and measured it with respect.

"One would have thought they made it for me," he said. "But how thick that steel is I cannot tell. It's as well we have fifty kilos for each."

They sat round in silence, watching him work and directing the beams of torches as he ordered. The socks which Rafael thought he had seen were indeed socks, slung closely together, feet downwards, from a canvas belt. The belt went barely halfway round the column, and El Vicario extended it with a second belt and more socks. When the circle was complete he filled each sock with four sticks of gelignite and ran a band round the lot so that the charge was in continuous contact with the steel.

"That is the necklace, mates. I shall now set the jewels in it — plenty to make sure."

He inserted detonators round the ring, connecting them with fuse and leaving a long tail of it free.

"The final task is dangerous," he said. "I recommend that you all go out and stand at a safe distance. I might, it's true, escape in the darkness, but why should I after all this work and two more wells to do? Besides, I do not know what arrangements you have made to get me clear of Cabo Desierto."

None of them thought of refusing. It was not so much that El Vicario had imposed himself as that they were awed by his meticulous handling of destruction and the sheer monstrosity of his objective.

Whatever he was doing did not take long. He opened the door of the hut just far enough to squeeze through and out, and shut it again.

"That one is now doomed," he said. "Do not go near it on any account until I tell you exactly what precautions you must take!"

So on along the ridge to 98 and 98A. El Vicario had no more ready-made belts or bands in his box and demanded string with which to tie his circle of gelignite between the flanges. They had none. Old wire was found but the exacting craftsman rejected it; wire was not pliable enough to hold the sticks in firm contact with each other and the steel. One of the men remarked diffidently that he had some fishing line at home, and El Vicario told him to run and get it. Rafael could not protest. There was no hurry. But what an absurdity to have material of every kind within reach except a simple ball of string!

El Vicario was unworried. He said little, never adding anything of his own to the blast of exasperated curses whispered into the dark whenever the strain of waiting became unbearable. Once he appeared to be dozing; once he accepted a pull at Rafael's bottle to pass the time. When the fishing line at last arrived, he took much longer than before to fit 98 and 98A with their necklaces, needing the hands of another man on the opposite side of the Christmas Tree. At both wells he insisted on adding his finishing touch alone, then slid out through the door of the hut and shut it behind him.

"And when will this go off?"

"Patience! Patience! When you like, Rafael, and not before. You have only to leave a couple of men outside each hut to see that no one comes near it."

"How far away should they be?"

"Near enough to keep off strangers. I tell you there is no risk."

"Do not forget that you must say clearly what we are to do if you want to get away alive!" Antón warned him.

"Mate, as I see it, Rafael will have my automatic in one hand and the boat's painter in the other. If he is not content with my very simple instructions, he can hardly miss me at that range."

It was now nearly four in the morning. The operation had taken far longer than El Vicario's estimate. Both the search for wire and the wait for the fishing line had run away with time, and movement in the dark had been slow. The men of the pickets on the Sentinels, except for those left on guard, went home by the usual road along the ridge while Rafael and Antón hurried El Vicario straight down the pipeline to the refinery. The dark labyrinth of tubes and cylinders, vertical and horizontal, linked by coils and bulbs of steel, dwarfed the three as if they were grubs in the viscera of a dead body and appealed to El Vicario's similar instinct for disintegration.

"Would not this have done, friend Rafael? And to think it is all full of gasses and liquids!"

Rafael was tired and for the first time more exasperated by El Vicario's character than admiring.

"No!" he replied angrily. "This? This is a toy! The wealth of the Company is in the ground. Keep moving if you want to be clear of the land by dawn!"

Up in the shacks behind the refinery cocks were already crowing. The boat was in the still basin, floating on polished night. El Vicario dropped into it and took stock of his food, water and fuel.

"Now start the engine, but do not throw the clutch or I fire!"

"Agreed, mate, agreed! Here is all you have to do. Throw open the door of a hut. You had better open all three simultaneously. This will break a small tube of acid — but you do not need a lecture on chemistry. Let me assure you that in ten minutes the acid will have eaten its way to other interesting substances which will then ignite, producing the same effect upon an end of fuse as — shall we say? — a lighted cigarette. Since the fuse is instantaneous, the result will also be so."

"So we have ten minutes only?"

"That is ample, friend Rafael. By then you will be too far away for the shock to affect you. But the concrete of the sheds might fly some distance, so take cover!"

"Good luck, Vicario! And thank you."

"A last favor. Might I have my pistol? Without it in such circumstances I am naked."

Rafael tossed it on to the floorboards as the propeller

swirled and the boat moved away. He watched it slide over the water of the port from streak to streak of light and turn for the entrance at full speed. The last seen of it was a scatter of foam as El Vicario met and mounted the first long roller of the Pacific.

"The devil! And now we have to climb up again," Rafael complained. "Antón, I thought it was all to be automatic and would go up while we were at breakfast."

"I don't like it. Ten minutes is not enough. And all this of chemistry — who knows?"

"He said there was no risk and he is not a man to lie."

"But he might wish to kill us all."

"What for, Antón?"

"Well, if you are satisfied, let's go! But I cannot climb up the pipeline after that night and an empty belly, Rafael."

"I am tired, too. We will go round by the road. The thing is done and an hour more or less does not matter."

At the Sentinels Rafael explained the procedure and asked for a volunteer to open the door of 98A. He himself would do 98, the middle Sentinel, and Antón 97. Both were to keep their eyes on him and open the doors when he raised his hand. All three would then run down the slope and take cover in dead ground below the ridge.

He did his best to reassure them, but himself was the only one who was confident. He had talked enough with El Vicario to be sure of just two qualities which he was capable of judging: the man's honesty and his conscientious work. The rest of him was a puzzle. He seemed to be an idealist of a sort, at war with all industrial society. Rafael did not agree that it was invariably to be condemned. Up to the murder of Catalina he had been, he remembered, happy.

As he walked up to 98 he was not afraid of the explosion or the unknown energy it would release, only of action that was irrevocable. The dawn was oppressive under the mountain shadow which shut off the coast and held it between mercy of night and clarity of day. Across the golf course, now perceptibly dark green, were the skeletons and rectangles of the old field, black against the colorless Andes. To the west Cabo Desierto was closed by the desolate silver plain of the Pacific. There was no way out.

The other two, to right and left, kept pace with him. Raising his hand he flung open the door of 98. Instinctively and in spite of his confidence he started to run, but stopped himself halfway down the slope and looked round. He was overcome by fury and disgust to see that Antón had only opened the door of 97 about as far as the crack by which El Vicario had let himself out. And this was the man who had killed with no necessity for it. A *bravo* without courage!

Well, but there were still most of the ten minutes left. The Company should not be presented with one well, good enough in itself to exploit all the oil in that reservoir four kilometers below. He pounded back up the slope, going straight for the even, metaled road between 97 and 98 along which he could run much faster. He had no watch but was sure he could reach 97 in three minutes.

When he got there he found that Antón had tentatively opened the door rather wider than El Vicario and had then lost his nerve. That was like him — to fight and to threaten but to be so afraid of the abnormal that he had neither obeyed nor quite disobeyed. Rafael could not be sure whether that tube of acid was broken or not, and even if he had known what to look for there was no time. He threw the door wide open to make certain and cleared off as fast as he could manage on legs which were failing and stumbling. 97 was farthest of all from the dead ground.

He heard the blast and fell flat, with a second in which to be consciously thankful that he was not hurt. Then there was a roaring in his ears and an instant of agony.

The roaring, far away, was still in his ears. He felt very light as if he could fly if he wanted to, but he could move only his head and his arms a little. He opened his eyes and saw the ceiling of the hospital and the face of Dr. Solano moving across it.

"Then I am alive, doctor?"

"For a little while, Rafael."

"This is it?"

"This is it."

"And Chepe?"

"On the way. When he heard the explosions he went out to find you."

"And Catalina? But I remember. Of course."

"Do you want a priest, Rafael?"

"No. Would Don Mateo speak to me?"

"He is here."

Mat had been startled from sleep by the first explosion. Before he was on his feet there were two more, close together. He assumed that El Vicario had double-crossed them all and blown the Charca. From his bedroom window he could see the east corner of the pool. The water was still and no fumes hung over it. He ran up to the roof of his house. A distant screaming roar, like the sound of a giant rocket except that it was level and continuous, left no doubt what had happened. The huts of the Three Sentinels had gone from the ridge; and again there were no fumes to be seen, only a curious dancing haze over the wells.

Where were the pillars of flame? Well, in war he had known enough of explosions and their effect. The air had probably been blown clear away, leaving a vacuum through which the column of oil had blasted, vaporizing as if in the jet of a monstrous carburetor. A spark from stone on steel or any friction whatever could light the gas at any moment.

His car would not start. There had been some advantage, after all, in being fetched by a chauffeur. It was the last straw. They could now add to their accusations that the General Manager had reached the scene after everyone else. Pepe and Amelia came out to push. When he told them as coolly as he could what had happened, Amelia burst into tears affecting Pepe in his turn.

His wrists were trembling, so he drove very carefully along the palm-lined avenue which he had had the conceit to call the ghetto. On the road to the Sentinels the Company ambulance passed him racing down to the hospital. He parked among a dozen cars at the side of the road a safe distance from 97 — if there was a safe distance. When he got out he could feel the ground shuddering under his feet.

Gulls were planing round and round the haze. Mat allowed them to fascinate him for there was nothing else he could face. Was the haze to their eyes some sort of sea with possible food in it, or were they trying to gain height on the up current which they felt must be present though the vapor prevented them from entering it?

Gateson came up — a strange Gateson, full of sympathy as one oilman to another.

"Who was it?" Mat asked.

"Garay, of course."

"How do you know?"

"Thorpe and Solano went out with a stretcher and brought him in. What for? They could have been roasted any minute."

Garay. Rafael Garay, whom he thought he had persuaded. This was the uttermost end of failure. Without any difference in the scream of the escaping oil, the haze above 98 passed through incandescence as quickly as a flash of sheet lightning. All three Sentinels were instantly turned to candles in the sky: giant Bunsen burners with the blue base of their yellow flames three hundred feet above the ground. The watchers threw up their arms to guard eyes from the heat of 97. The wings of the gulls caught fire. They plummeted to the ground, black, lifeless meteorites.

Without another word to anyone Mat got into his car and drove down to the hospital. There was nothing to be done, nothing ever to be done unless those incredible Texas specialists could cap the wells. One, yes. Two, possibly. But three, with only a space of four hundred yards between one and another? Henry Constantinides and Dave Gunner, for once agreeing, might not consider the attempt worthwhile and so hand over the field to those prospective buyers for anything they liked to offer.

He sat in the waiting room. The matron believed the case to be hopeless, since Solano had given no orders for the operating theater to be prepared or for the Company plane. He was with the patient; he would be told at once that the General Manager was there.

Luis Solano came out of the casualty ward.

"He wants to see you, Mateo."

"Any hope?"

"None. He knows it. He's all flat below the waist. We had to push a concrete panel off him."

"That was superb, Luis."

"Why? We couldn't leave him there. He must have had helpers but they had all run away."

"Chepe?"

"They found him curled up on the hillside calling for both of you. A car has gone to fetch him. Come!"

The dark face on the pillow was neither afraid nor triumphant. It seemed to hold only acceptance of what it had done in the world and for what it must die. A priest, Mat thought, could not have made a better job of it than Rafael himself.

"I am sorry, Don Mateo, but there was nothing else."

"It may be that there was nothing else, Rafael."

"They will send you away?"

"They will."

"You will be very much alone, Don Mateo."

"That is nothing new for me."

"By God, it is nothing new for any man who is a man!"

"Quiet, Rafael!"

"Let me speak while I can! When you go, will you take my son with you?"

"Willingly, if you wish it. But we shall need a piece of paper."

"You are right. A piece of paper. A man cannot be born

or die or eat without a piece of paper. Fetch the Mayor quickly, brother! I will not allow myself to die until he comes. But there is a roaring in my ears."

"In mine, too. It is nothing, brother, and without importance."